The Four Corners

SHINE-A-LIGHT
PRESS

Visit Shine-A-Light Press on our website:
www.ShineALightPress.com
on Twitter: @SALPress
And on Facebook: www.facebook.com/SALPress

Visit The Four Corners on our website:
www.TheFourCornersBooks.com
on Twitter: @4CornersTrilogy
And on Facebook: www.facebook.com/TheFourCornersBook

Visit C.S. Elston on his website:
www.cselston.com
on Twitter: @cselston
And on Facebook: www.facebook.com/cselston

The Shine-A-Light Press logo is a trademark of Shine-A-Light Corp.

The Four Corners
Copyright © 2015 by Christopher Scott Elston

Second edition printed February, 2020

Publisher's Note: *The Four Corners* is a work of fiction. Where real people, events, establishments, organizations, or locales appear, they are used fictitiously. All other elements of the novel are drawn from the author's imagination and any resemblance to actual persons or events is coincidental.

Scripture quotations are taken from *The Holy Bible, New International Version,* Copyright © 1973, 1978, 1984 by International Bible Society.

Book Layout and Cover Illustration by Joe Ingalls: JoeIngallsDesign.com

Illustrations by Madison McClean

Author's Photo by Christie Bruno

ISBN 978-0-692-43551-9

Library of Congress Control Number: 2015906519

Printed in the U.S.A.
U.S.A. $15.99

For my family, whose confidence, love and support allowed me to take many steps of faith on the road to becoming the man I was created to be.

Still walking. . .

Acknowledgments

I would like to extend my deepest gratitude to my original proofreaders: My parents, Doug and Judy; my father-in-law, Craig; and my wife, Andrea. They have all been supportive in numerous ways, not the least of which is having read drafts of the book before publication and offering valuable feedback. My dad, in particular, has been my greatest grammar coach starting way back when. As a child, I would leave him notes to tell him I loved him when I had to go to bed before he got home from working late and asked him to correct them to make me a better writer. Andrea, a fantastic educator of twenty years, also helped me by creating the educational literary unit and helping me to create the faith-based study that are each available as a free download on "The Four Corners" pages of both ShineALightPress.com and cselston.com.

Thank you to Heritage Christian Academy in Bothell, Washington for allowing me to test the book out in a couple of your classrooms during the editing process. The suggestions from both teachers and students were quite fun and also very helpful.

I would like to further offer a warm 'thank you' to my niece, Madison McClean, for providing her beautiful artwork for the interior of this book. I adore the images the story inspired her to draw and am grateful for the opportunity to share them with everyone who reads this book.

Appreciation also has to be extended to Joe Ingalls who did the beautiful cover illustration and jacket design as well as the layout for this book. His hard work makes mine shine brighter than it otherwise would have.

Finally, sincere gratitude goes out to Liana who, for this second edition, picked up where Joe left off.

Table of Contents

Part One *Of Interest*

Part Two *The Disappearance*

Part Three *The Awakening*

Part Four *A New Beginning*

Part Five *Pushing Through*

Part Six *Shared Struggle*

Part Seven *The Gathering*

Reader's Guide

The
Four Corners

C.S. Elston

PART ONE
Of Interest

CHAPTER ONE
Kinsey

Kinsey Snyder wasn't a particularly interesting nine-year-old boy. Maybe this was because he didn't seem to have any real interests. He didn't have a favorite musical group, book, super hero, movie or even television show. He didn't belong to any clubs or teams. He didn't sing either solo or in a choir, act in any plays, or play any musical instruments. He didn't participate in class or, really even recess for that matter, and he didn't have any true friends. Instead, he lived a relatively lonely life of self-imposed inaccessibility.

Kinsey even looked ordinary. He was of about average height for his age, just slightly over-weight, and appeared a little bit on the sloppy side. He even wore neutral colors and on the rare occasion that his clothes included any patterns, they were quite subtle. At some point in the not-too-distant past, Kinsey had simply stopped caring about the way he looked and it showed, but only slightly. If it showed too much, that would be interesting. Instead, nothing Kinsey said or did ever really stood out. And, nothing he chose to keep hidden ever really stood out either. No, Kinsey Snyder most definitely was not interesting.

Of course, this wasn't the way Kinsey wished his life to be. It just so happened that this is the way it was. He wanted friends but he was too afraid to make them. He knew many of the answers to the questions his teacher asked but was too worried that if he finally raised his hand he would somehow say it wrong and be laughed at by the other kids. He wished he knew how to play the guitar but, he didn't want to ask his parents for lessons because then they would know if it turned out he wasn't any good. He wanted to be athletic but he was terrified that if he played at recess, he would be picked last when everyone was divided into teams. Then, in order to make the situation even worse, his deep fear was that he would prove all of them right for doing so by dropping the ball or throwing it to the wrong team or some other stupid thing. So, it had become easier for Kinsey to just not try. Not trying had recently developed into a theme for his entire life.

Although Kinsey didn't realize it yet, not trying is worse than failing. Failure is a chance to learn how to succeed. Not trying is the acceptance of a life where success will never be possible. He had no way of knowing, but soon Kinsey would find himself in a situation where he would have to change course and try something bigger than anything he'd ever been faced with - even bigger than anything he'd ever imagined. And, the stakes associated with both success and failure in the situation Kinsey would soon be facing would affect the rest of his life. In fact, that unforeseen situation would put that very future at risk. Kinsey was about to face an unimaginable matter of life or death that would change everything he had ever known.

Until then, however, Kinsey would continue to live an isolated life of self-defeat. On that rare occasion when someone did ask him to play something, Kinsey would just shake his head as if silently saying "No, thank you." Because of this, people had mostly stopped asking.

Similarly, if his teacher called on him, Kinsey would merely shrug his shoulders as if silently telling her "I don't know the answer" – even though he probably did. As a result, Mrs. Shilley had stopped calling on him in order to protect him from embarrassment. She had talked to his parents, tried to talk to him and even tried to get him to talk to the school counselor. So far, nothing had even remotely improved the situation. For all intents and purposes, by not trying at anything else, Kinsey was subconsciously trying to make himself invisible – and he was doing a pretty good job of it.

Having essentially withdrawn from the world and into

himself, Kinsey Snyder had become almost completely silent in the presence of anyone other than the person solely responsible for keeping his sanity alive: his sister. The otherwise silent life that Kinsey had chosen to lead was stirring up some strong emotions. Emotions are powerful forces, capable of destroying lives or saving them, generating peace and grace or causing fights and even wars.

Emotions can only stay bottled up for so long. The consistent choice to stay silent meant that emotions had been building inside of Kinsey like lava in a volcano for quite some time and it wouldn't be long before they just had to erupt out of him.

But, for now, Kinsey sat in the back of the classroom in his chair with a desk attached to it, which made it immobile and totally uncomfortable. In fact, if Kinsey had been a more imaginative boy, he might have pictured it being made in a dungeon by a bitter old man who hated children and wanted to find ways to slowly torture them. As much as he hated that chair/desk combination, however, Kinsey's mind was elsewhere as he found himself staring at the clock – silently and without drawing any attention to himself whatsoever, of course.

As was usual at the end of the school day, Kinsey had nearly forgotten there were even other kids in the room and had completely tuned the teacher out. Mrs. Shilley had started to recap the day, as if he and his forgotten classmates hadn't already experienced it with her, but Kinsey didn't hear a word of it. Instead, he had turned his attention to the second hand on the clock above the whiteboard. He followed it with a slight head-nod like someone jamming to the beat of his favorite song flowing out of a set of headphones that only he could hear. Kinsey, however, was simply counting down the seconds until the final bell, the bell that announced his freedom.

To him, that bell somehow sounded different than the other bells that he heard throughout the day. The first bell, the one that began the school day, was absolutely the worst. But, then they somehow improved as the day progressed. The final bell actually managed to sound chipper, genuinely happy even, like a bird fresh from slumber stepping up onto the edge of its nest and bending its legs while raising its wings, ready to take flight. To Kinsey, it was a glorious sound. So, counting the seconds until he heard that magnificent ring had become a habit starting sometime the year before.

Maybe it was because he was happy to be done with the school day. Maybe it was because he was going home where he could sit in his room and not be bothered. But, more than likely, it was because it announced his favorite part of the day: his walk home with the only person he ever really wanted to talk to. She was his very favorite person in the entire world and, luckily, the one who was always waiting for him when he got out of school. She was his older sister Tatum and, unlike Kinsey, she was very interesting.

CHAPTER TWO
Tatum

What made Tatum Snyder so interesting wasn't some magical power or incredible talent. Nor was it a long list of awards or accomplishments. She wasn't even particularly creative or inventive. She was, however, quite inspirational. The old saying about people who are handed lemons by life but somehow manage to make lemonade, described Tatum in a nutshell.

Tatum was smack dab in the middle of most of the same trials and misfortunes that Kinsey was. But, her ability to face reality head-on made her quite different from her younger brother. And, it showed in nearly everything that she did.

Tatum actually liked school and she had always demonstrated it by participating both in class and on the playground. She never watched the clock the way Kinsey did because she was genuinely engaged in whatever the teacher was saying. Not that Tatum didn't enjoy their after-school walk home together but, school was much more fun than being at home, especially since she had finally advanced to junior high this year.

Not surprisingly, she had embraced her new surroundings, and all of the challenges they provided, with grit and enthusiasm. Her good grades remained steady as always and she loved the fact that she was given the opportunity to learn from five teachers each day instead of just the one per year in elementary school. Furthermore, she had managed to hold on to her old friends while, at the same time, making new ones.

Also in contrast to her younger brother, Tatum took pride in the way she looked and, had therefore taken on a nearly regal appearance. She got up early in the morning and spent time choosing and then ironing her clothes, fixing her hair just the way she wanted it, and even applying just a hint of make-up.

Being the mature, reliable girl that she was, Tatum had begun to take over a lot of motherly responsibilities since her mom had decided to start selling houses. She did some of the household chores and often ordered dinner from one of the local restaurants that delivered. But, the main thing Tatum had taken over was caring for Kinsey. She made sure he was ready for school in the morning, helped him with his homework at night, and with pretty much everything else he was supposed to do in between.

Tatum would have enjoyed more free time to be social and possibly even join one of the sports teams at her school but, for the most part, she was okay with the role she had taken on at home. Someone had to do it. Truth be known, she believed the job belonged to one of her parents. Likely, her mom since it had been hers to begin with. Her mom had never officially quit, but she had slowly stopped doing the job and someone needed to pick up the slack. Tatum was there to do it. Sure, there was a bit of resulting frustration with her mother hidden underneath Tatum's calm and collected exterior but such was life and Tatum embraced it with the same vigor that she embraced everything else.

That kind of responsibility might be too much for most twelve year-old girls but Tatum was not like most twelve year-old girls. She was stable, healthy, and didn't suffer from wide mood swings. She was the kind of girl who recognized problems, generated options, made choices, and followed through. While Kinsey had turned into a human tortoise, hiding in his shell, Tatum had transformed into a human cheetah, sprinting with purpose. That is what made Tatum Snyder so interesting.

Her life wasn't ideal, but she had the aptitude to make the most of the way things were. Instead of grumbling about the time she spent taking care of her brother when she could be hanging out with her friends, she enjoyed his company and put the energy she would have wasted grumbling into making sure she took care of him the best that she possibly could.

On this day and at this hour, Tatum found herself where she usually did. Her school let out twenty minutes earlier than her brother's. So, she would gather the things she was taking home, walk two blocks to the elementary school, sit on the front steps below the branches of the tall maple tree, and read.

She had recently been assigned to read *A Wrinkle in Time* by Madeleine L'Engle. It was no trouble getting into the characters in the book because it involved a girl and her little brother, to which Tatum could easily relate, even though the characters were quite different from Kinsey and herself. In the story, a stranger had appeared at their door claiming to have been blown off course and then explained that there was such a thing as a wrinkle in space and time called a *tesseract* and it was through this wrinkle that they could travel on a quest to find their father who had been missing for more than a year. Tatum was thrilled by the adventure and thankful for the selection made by her English teacher, Mrs. Chadwick. She could hardly wait to see where the story took her.

Therefore, as she sat in the shade provided by the large maple tree, she reached into her school bag, dug around until she found the book, pulled it out, opened it to her bookmark and began to read. She had to move quickly because the school bell would be ringing shortly and she knew from experience that Kinsey would be at her side only moments later.

She looked forward to seeing her little brother but she also treasured the opportunity to read quietly. Reading itself was a wonderful escape for Tatum but this was also a moment to herself, a break from the chaos of everyday life in this world but, more specifically, from the chaos that existed in the Snyder family. This was a moment of peace and calm. It was a brief moment but one that Tatum looked forward to every single day.

Tatum could have chosen to catch up on any homework during this moment but she very nearly always chose to read the novels that she had been assigned in her English class. The rare exception was when she had a test the next day in a subject where she didn't feel she otherwise had enough time to be fully prepared. On any other day, this was always a moment when she could enjoy the relaxation of dipping into the pages of a great story.

Just as the children in *A Wrinkle in Time* were about to be transported to another planet, that annoying school bell rang and Tatum was forced to slide her bookmark back in between the pages where she left off, stuff the book back into her school bag, zip the bag closed, and stand ready to greet her brother.

CHAPTER THREE
Just Kids

For Kinsey, the final school bell was a personal symbol of liberty. As such, when it began to ring, it started the fastest movement of his day. The habitually slow-moving nine-year-old boy could snap his book shut or gather his papers and have everything in his backpack, with no need to stop at his locker, and be on his way out the classroom door before the ringing stopped. He was almost always the first person to exit the building. Not because he prided himself on it or found some sense of achievement in it, but because he couldn't wait to get to the one moment in each day where he actually felt just a hint of joy.

For Tatum, the same bell ended the most tranquil few minutes she had in a day. She barely had enough time to pack back up and get to her feet as her focus shifted from relaxation to Kinsey. But, for her, human cheetah mode was always in full effect.

Therefore, as they met up in their usual spot at the bottom of the Ronald Reagan Elementary School front steps to begin their journey home, their easy conversation immediately kicked into gear.

"Hey, buddy," Tatum greeted Kinsey. "How was your day?"

The sky looked as though God had poured out a giant container of the deepest blue paint in the universe and then cranked the sun's intensity up to the maximum setting to make sure no one missed it. Only, Kinsey was so focused on seeing his sister, he actually failed to notice.

"Okay," Kinsey responded with a shrug. "How was yours?"

"Good," Tatum said. "I got an A- on my science test. How'd you do on your math quiz?"

"B," Kinsey responded a bit sheepishly.

"Not too bad," Tatum said, trying to encourage him. "We'll keep working on it. Long division confused me a little in fourth grade, too. Plus, Mrs. Shilley is a stickler for making you show your work."

"No kidding," Kinsey said as he cracked a slight smile, appreciating his sister's support, and they walked in silence for a moment until the smile faded. It happened just as they turned the corner at Orchard Avenue and started down Strawberry Street. This was the landmark they reached each school day where

Kinsey realized that they would be home sooner than he wanted to be. Not wanting to be either at school or at home, he wished that walk could last a bit longer. In fact, if he had the option of gaining a magical power, he'd choose the one that would allow him to stretch those streets out until blocks became miles just to make that walk last an hour or two. That longer walk would be enough to make the whole day worth his while.

Noticing Kinsey's faded smile, Tatum tried to keep the conversation going. "What kind of homework do you have?"

"Math, geography, and spelling."

"Need me to quiz you on anything?"

"Maybe spelling and geography," Kinsey thought out loud, "but not until later. Like, after dinner. So I can try to get it down myself first. Then maybe you can help me figure out the new math stuff after that."

"Okay," she responded as she scheduled the evening in her head. "We can do it around seven or seven-thirty then."

"Sure," Kinsey agreed. Another moment of silence allowed Kinsey's mind to drift back to where they were heading. "Think mom's home?" he finally asked.

"Doubtful," Tatum responded. "I heard her on the phone this morning saying something about an open house. I'm sure she'll be home by dinner though. Those things are usually over by four. Especially when they have them on weekdays instead of weekends or evenings."

"About the same time as dad then," Kinsey said before laying on the sidewalk. "Great. Let the games begin."

Tatum looked at her brother, sympathetically, as he stared at the sidewalk in front of his shuffling feet. She felt the pain, too. She had just been born with a little better equipment with which to handle it. She decided to try and make a joke out of it by saying, "They do almost make a sport out of it, don't they? Like a couple of Olympians."

"More like gladiators," Kinsey insisted.

"You're right," Tatum agreed as she realized this was something no one could really make a joke out of. "More like gladiators."

They stopped out in front of their house and Kinsey watched as Tatum opened the mailbox and pulled the mail out. He was deep in thought and working the courage up to ask a big question.

"Do you think they're going to get a divorce?" Kinsey finally blurted out.

"Maybe," Tatum responded. "I hope not. But, the way things have been going lately, I don't know. They only seem to be getting worse."

"Yeah," Kinsey sadly agreed. They walked toward the front door while Kinsey collected the courage to get the next question out. Finally, as Tatum dug her keys out of the side pocket of her school bag and used them to unlock the door, he did. "What'll happen to us if they do?"

"Hey," Tatum blurted out as she pushed the door open and pulled her keys back out of the lock. She turned and grabbed Kinsey by both shoulders so she could look him in the eyes. "Nothing will ever separate us."

"But, what if we don't have a choice? We're just kids."

"We always have a choice and I will always choose you."

"What about courts and lawyers and judges and all of that stuff? We can't do anything about that," Kinsey exclaimed with tears in his eyes.

"There's always a way," Tatum reassured him. "Even if we got separated temporarily, we'll always find a way to wind up back together. I promise. Okay?"

"Okay," said Kinsey, feeling just a little better.

"Now get upstairs and do your homework," she told him. "I'll bring dinner up when it's ready and then you'll have about an hour left to prepare for the hot seat."

"Hot seat?"

"Yeah, the hot seat. My quizzing you on spelling and geography."

"Oh, right."

"So get going," Tatum said as they stepped inside and she shut the door behind them.

Kinsey, back to his more typical speed, walked slowly up the stairs as Tatum set her bag down and started flipping through the mail. She quickly realized that there was really nothing of importance to her. Of course, her mind wasn't really on the mail anyway. She was more focused on the promise she had made to her brother. She had promised him that nothing would keep them apart and she meant it with every fiber of her being.

However, neither of them could possibly understand just how hard that promise would be to keep and that the forces working against them were far greater than anything that had ever crossed their minds. The burst of emotion that would finally soon spew out of Kinsey would bring about circumstances they couldn't possibly foresee. In fact, no one in the Snyder family was aware of how difficult things were about to get and the least suspecting member was the most distracted person: Tatum and Kinsey's mother, Jill.

CHAPTER FOUR
Jill

Although every bit as physically, fashionably, and mentally put together as her daughter, Jill Snyder's life had always been full of distractions. She started out as Jill Wagner but met Grant Snyder in high school. She was a cheerleader and he played football and basketball so, she fell in love watching him play his sports and hanging out with him after the games.

He wasn't the best player out there but, he was pretty good and she could tell it was primarily because he labored so hard at it. His good looks and natural charm didn't hurt, but that strong work ethic was the first quality that captivated her. After all, she was a hard worker, too. Good grades were very important to Jill and, although she was naturally bright, she put in the over-time to ensure she remained among the top students in her class.

A strong drive, however, was one of the very few qualities that Jill and Grant had in common. In fact, the many ways in which they proved that opposites definitely do attract were far greater in number. She was a girly-girl and embodied everything that came with it while he was about as manly as a teenage boy could be.

Grant was Jill's first major distraction.

They went to college together intending to get married as soon as they graduated but, they were so in love with each other that they decided they couldn't wait that long. Toward the end of their freshman year, they began to plan a wedding and got married the summer after their sophomore year.

They both intended to finish school but, half way through their junior year, Jill found out that she was already pregnant with Tatum. This was a terrifying and yet thrilling time for them. The thought of having their own family was a source of intense excitement and joy.

They spent countless hours talking about what they loved about the families they grew up in and what traditions they wanted to continue. For example, Jill had grown up driving nearly four hours to get to a lake on the other side of the Cascade Mountain Range where her family spent a week every summer. Lake Chelan was a tradition she absolutely wanted to continue. Grant had no problem with that and they had every intention of keeping that up.

They also spent a significant amount of time discussing the things they were adamant about doing differently. For example,

Jill had a father whom she loved dearly. He was a good man and a hard worker. It's probably the genetic gene pool from which she got her drive. However, that drive caused him to miss a lot of birthdays and recitals when she was growing up. That was something she and Grant intended to do differently. They were determined that they would always have time for each other and for both the child they were having and any additional children they eventually had. She was determined that, that priority was going to be a new and improved tradition in the family she and Grant were creating together.

Although the responsibility of having a brand new human being who was completely dependent on them for their every single need scared both Jill and Grant like crazy, the fear was outweighed by the adventure of it all. And, they were determined to make it a great adventure.

Kids were Jill's second major distraction.

Love and family are two of the best kinds of distractions people can experience. Unfortunately, not all distractions are positive.

After eight or nine years of being a terrific wife and a wonderful mother, Jill began to experience doubts about her adequacy as a woman. She looked up to women with great careers as positive role models and she started wondering if she had sold herself short by not finishing college and starting a career.

Life is made up of choices and the consequences, either positive or negative, of those choices. Jill choosing to love Grant resulted in the addition of even more love to her life in the form of a husband and children. That was a good choice and a positive consequence.

However, distractions, like life, come with choices and consequences. While creating a family resulted in positive consequences, Jill had entered a time in her life when many of her major choices were resulting in negative consequences. And, unfortunately, she was not their only victim.

Doubt was her third major distraction.

As the doubts snowballed and began to take control of Jill's life, she tried to fix them by volunteering for charities, taking classes, and eventually, getting her real estate broker's license. Choosing to better one's self is a noble thing but ignoring existing responsibilities because you've decided to add new ones can create a dump truck full of problems. In other words, Jill's newly self-imposed distractions began to crowd the original ones out of her life, which ultimately made things more difficult for her because she was losing sight of the positive distractions she once cherished.

These new distractions often led to fights with Grant and made both Tatum and Kinsey feel ignored. The more Jill did things solely for herself, the more unsettled her family became.

And, the more unsettled, and therefore unhappy, the family became, the more she resented them for not letting her be who she wanted to be.

However, without realizing it had happened, she had become a lot like her dad. Like him, she was a good person. But, also like him, she had become so driven that she was missing out on a very important part of life.

In fact, while she mentally justified her actions by the fact that she made it to every birthday, she was no longer as present as she told herself she was. She often went outside to make or take phone calls in the middle of cake and ice cream or the opening of gifts. And, the tradition of going to Lake Chelan started to fade, when Jill decided she didn't have time for a vacation because summer was the busy season for residential real estate. Chelan was something her dad had never missed. This meant that, in some ways, she had become an even worse version of something she had once vowed not to tolerate in her own family.

So, there she was, a real estate agent with a family at home who didn't even realize how good she was at it. And, she really was good. She had always been a flirtatious woman and it benefited her in her new occupation. Let's face it, when a couple bought a house, the woman typically had to be the most impressed with it but, the house itself was pretty much out of

Jill's control. The ability to boost the man's ego, however, was within Jill's control and she was excellent at doing it in a tactful way that didn't threaten the man's wife. This came in very handy. After all, the man was often the one signing the check. And, today she got one step closer to a very big check.

As she pulled into her driveway, she was completely focused on all of the little things that had to be done in the next twenty-four hours in order to ensure that this deal closed the next day at 2:00 p.m. She turned the ignition off, gathered up all of her things from inside the car, and rushed into the house without so much as a thought about seeing her family or the fact that dinner-time was looming.

CHAPTER FIVE
Matriarchs

Both the side-by-side refrigerator and freezer doors were open wide as Tatum went back and forth between the two, rummaging through the various condiments, both regular and decaffeinated frozen coffee beans, breads of nearly every kind, random one-offs like key lime pie flavored yogurt and an orange, three different types of ice cream and about a half dozen flavors of popsicles – about a third of which were badly freezer burned. *There's quite a bit here,* she thought as she heard the sound of her mother's arrival coming from the garage. *But none of it adds up to an actual meal. I'll be flipping through take-out menus in five... four... three... two...*

Hurriedly entering the kitchen, Jill was immediately greeted by Tatum who popped her head out of the cool air and closed the freezer door. "Hey. Just in time."

"Yeah?" Jill asked as she walked right past her daughter,

paying a minimal amount of attention. "What am I just in time for, honey?"

"Figuring out dinner," Tatum said as she closed the refrigerator door. "I was just hunting for any and all available leftovers."

"What'd you find?" Jill asked.

"Nothing that works," Tatum groaned. "That's why you're just in time to rescue us from certain starvation."

Jill walked back over to Tatum as she dug through her wallet. Finally, she found what she was looking for and handed it to Tatum. "Wish granted," she said.

"What's this?" Tatum inquired, knowing the answer but asking just to hear her mom's response anyway. She took the white credit card and then watched her mom turn to leave.

"Dinner," Jill responded. "Order something and have it delivered. Just make sure there's plenty for all four of us. I'll be in my office. I have a ton of work to do."

What else is new? Tatum thought sarcastically to herself as she attempted to keep a feeling of bitterness from settling into her heart. She couldn't keep it out completely though. A dash sprinkled its way in every night around this time.

As promised, Jill disappeared into her office completely unaware of just how routine this scenario had become. It wasn't that Jill disliked her family or didn't want to spend time with her kids. It was that a bitterness of her own had seeped into her heart in response to the resentment she felt from her family for the decision she had made to go back to work. It made her more determined to show how good she was at her new job because she thought that they might actually begin to understand and appreciate what she was doing if she could just prove that she was doing it well. This determination made her blind to the effect she was having. The more distant she became, the worse the situation got. The worse the situation got, the more determined she became. And, although she was not aware of it, the more determined she became, the more distant she got – starting the blind downward spiral all over again.

Tatum, on the other hand, was very aware as she went to the kitchen drawer near the phone and started digging through a ridiculously large stack of take out menus just as she had silently predicted she would be doing.

Tatum, of course, would have preferred for things to be quite different. She loved the idea of cooking something with her mom. Kinsey could even join them if he wanted to – which he probably wouldn't. Her mom used to cook all of the time when she and Kinsey were younger and she was very good at it. They had yummy homemade meals four or five times a week back then. Tatum's personal favorite was her mom's homemade clam chowder. At this point, Tatum would have happily settled for one or two nights a week. Heck, the clam chowder could even come from a can for all she cared. Any other version of dinner at home would've been better than this one.

Or, instead of cooking, the four of them could even go out to eat together at a real sit-down restaurant. Of course, for that to be enjoyable, her parents would have to get along. Or, at least be civil. Heck, they wouldn't even have to talk to one another to make it a far more desirable situation than her current reality. But, this was the way things were.

Reality was Tatum putting dinner together each night from groceries her mom brought home or the previous night's leftovers. Or, even more common was ordering something to be delivered. Once in a great while, one of her parents brought something home from a fast food restaurant. But, that was rare because they had convinced themselves that take out was a healthier option. While that might technically be true for the body, Tatum was smart enough to know that this wasn't any healthier for their minds or their souls. The truth is her reality was also a house where it seemed like she and Kinsey were the only two people who really talked to one another. Unfortunately, there was absolutely no sign of her reality changing any time soon.

So, she continued flipping through the menus. She skipped all of the pizza places because she was sick-to-death of pizza, which six months ago she never would have thought was even possible. Pizza had always been a favorite in the Snyder house. Of course, to make things more complicated, they all liked different kinds. Her dad was a straight up pepperoni man. Just pepperoni wasn't enough for her brother, however, who liked a full-on meat extravaganza. Her mom liked the fancier stuff on her pizza pies like spinach, basil, garlic chunks, artichoke hearts, and white sauce. Tatum, on the other hand, could handle any of it but her favorite was a Hawaiian style pizza with Canadian bacon and pineapple. Maybe some red onion and red pepper flakes just to spice things up and add a little color to the pie. Everyone had their own unique favorites, but pizza in and of itself was a common ground for the Snyders. Unfortunately, she was burned out on all of it at that point, common ground or not.

What she really wanted right then was Mexican food, but she didn't know of a Mexican restaurant that delivered. *Might not be a bad idea for a business later on down the road,* she thought to herself. *Tacos To Go* or, *Burritos On The Run. Burritos On The Run would probably get made fun of. People would call us Burritos Give You The Runs,* she chuckled quietly. *Tacos To Go it is.*

Finally, she landed on a menu she hadn't ordered from in a while. She pulled it out, placed it on the counter, and started scanning the items while considering everyone and their assorted taste buds.

The hungriest member of the family was also the pickiest. Additionally, he was perhaps the only person more sensitive to and more disturbed by the family's routine than Tatum and Kinsey. He was the pepperoni pizza-loving family patriarch, Grant.

CHAPTER SIX
Grant

'The Brick' - that was Grant Snyder's nickname from early in his childhood. Almost everyone, including his parents, still called him 'The Brick'. His immediate family was the one exception. Jill was the only one who called him Grant and both Tatum and Kinsey, of course, called him 'Dad.'

His average height, coupled with the athletic build he still sported at almost 40 years of age made for a good-looking, stocky framed man who dressed well because he felt he should as a businessman, not because he wanted to.

The nickname, however, was not simply the result of his stocky build. Grant was always a rough-housing, activity-loving, tough-guy. He loved sports, cars, and being outdoors. He was ambitious, audacious, and strong-willed, qualities which served him well. He excelled in sports because of his hard work rather than some God-given talent, and that carried over into adulthood.

He dated quite a few girls in the first couple years of high school and began to develop a reputation as a "playa." But, that all changed when he got to know Jill. It didn't take long before he knew that was it for him. He fell in love fast and hard with this beautiful girl who had a quick wit, big brain, and fun-loving personality. He decided quickly that she was the only girl he ever wanted to be with again. He was thrilled to marry her during college and, quite frankly, he was just as thrilled when she told him she was pregnant. He wanted to be the guy taking care of his family. He viewed that as his job and it was one he was happy to take on. He told everyone that his family meant the world to him and he truly believed it.

When he finished college, he combined his experience working in a camping supply store with his business degree and opened his own sporting goods store. It turned into a successful business with four locations and potentially a fifth one approximately a year away. This meant a lot of hours and a lot of trips out of town for conferences and meetings with suppliers. As a result, he missed too many birthdays and anniversaries, which he ultimately realized wasn't going unnoticed. He also knew that this was something he and Jill had agreed would never happen before Tatum was born and it broke his heart to go back on his word but he truly didn't know how to avoid it and still keep the business running smoothly.

Grant did take notice of the fact that Jill was understanding about his absence when it had first started to happen. After all, she wanted him to be successful. Not just because she wanted the income that came with it but, she truly wanted it for him. She believed in him and his tenacious ways and felt like he deserved the success because he had earned it.

Once the absence had become a regular occurrence, Grant assumed, Jill most likely felt that it was too late to say anything at all. As the business grew, Grant's absence snowballed. And, it was something they had never spoken about. Grant felt guilt, and he assumed, Jill felt animosity.

When Jill decided to go back to work, Grant felt betrayed. He convinced himself that she was taking over part of his job and forcing him to take on part of hers. They weren't having financial troubles so it just didn't make any sense to him. He couldn't understand how she could do this to him without even asking how he felt about it. They started to fight a lot. Antagonism and sullenness began to replace love in their relationship.

She was very good at her job in the same way that he was good at what he did. Even though he could see that, he wouldn't admit it to her. After all, she had also been very good at being a wife and mother and he didn't understand why that wasn't enough for her. He also couldn't understand why Jill was willing to do this to the family that they had created together. In his mind, she was clearly wrong and his anger was absolutely just.

Grant "The Brick" Snyder found himself where he often did at this time of night during the week – sitting in his car, parked in the driveway. He loved his kids but his frustrations with Jill had made it difficult to come home. Nights were typically spent either, apart in silence or, up close and personal, screaming in each other's faces. Tonight, he would experience a little bit of both.

Deep down inside his soul, Grant knew that he still loved his wife. He certainly loved who she used to be. And, he privately hoped that person was still in there somewhere. He just found it increasingly difficult to imagine because he felt he hadn't seen her in a long time. He missed her terribly and, the blame, he felt, was rightly placed on this new person who had replaced the woman he married.

What Grant failed to realize was that everyone goes through changes. He had changed some over the years, too. But, the basic make-up of who a person is usually stays the same. They can't change how their body, mind and soul were created. Nor can they change where they come from. People can mask those things either on purpose or without even trying, but they can never hide them completely.

The things that do in fact change from time to time can be

either bad or good. People can become addicted to things that take over their lives and destroy them, or they can conquer those same addictions. People can become lazy or careless and waste their lives, or they can find purpose and become more productive and make a positive difference in the world at large or in their small community. People can grow selfish or rancorous. They can grow more loving and kind. People can become hostile and unforgiving. They can also become sympathetic and offer grace.

In short, some things are impossible to change. The things that are changeable can be either destructive or constructive. While Jill may have thought she was making a positive change in her life, the way in which she went about it created a negative environment for the people she truly did care about most and the vicious cycle had finally spun out of control. Instead of looking at it from her point of view and trying to understand what it was that caused the inner void she was trying to fill, Grant couldn't see past his feeling of betrayal and he had finally reached his breaking point. Sadly, everyone in the Snyder household had reached that point.

Home is meant to be a sanctuary: a place of solace, peace, and most of all, love. For Grant, home had become a dreaded place of provocation, turmoil, and most of all, resentment. He imagined the entire family probably felt much the same way he did. But, that didn't offer any comfort. It only made him angrier.

After waiting for as long as he felt he could, he knew it was his duty to head on inside and endure another round. So, he finally mustered up the courage to climb out of the car and start toward the house to do just that.

PART TWO
The Disappearance

CHAPTER SEVEN
Divided We Fall

Family time had essentially ceased to exist in the Snyder household and this night was no exception. It was a typical Tuesday night in early November, a night which painted a perfect picture of how truly absent any trace of unity had become.

A traditional family dinner, usually prepared by one or both parents, often the mom, is typically shared around a table without the distraction of any electronic devices. Instead, these are replaced with live conversation between family members with topics bouncing from subject to subject. It might start with "What did you do today?" and spread to some variation of sports, school, work, the possible existence of life on other planets, or even the latest adventures of SpongeBob Squarepants. But, family dinners at the Snyder house were far from traditional.

Tonight, Tatum had ordered dinner from Happy Feast, a

local Chinese restaurant she had called at least a half dozen times in the past. They were delivering Chicken Chow Mein, Vegetable Fried Rice, Kung Pao San Yan, and Cream Cheese Crab Fried Wontons.

When Happy Feast's deliveryman rang the doorbell, not surprisingly, Tatum was the one who answered. "Hi," she greeted him warmly.

"Hello," the short and squatty deliveryman with a head full of white hair replied while letting loose a smile that would spray sunshine into the darkest of places. "I just need a signature."

"One second," Tatum responded as she grabbed the food and the receipt from the man and spun around toward the kitchen having absorbed a bit of the deliveryman's cheerfulness. "Mom!" she yelled toward Jill's home office. "You need to sign the guy's receipt!"

Jill popped out of her methodically organized home office while continuing a conversation, through her cell phone's Bluetooth earpiece, in which she was attempting to politely convince a seller that he had overpriced his house. She appeared just long enough to grab the receipt from Tatum's hand, sign the restaurant copy, hand it off to the deliveryman, and close the door before promptly returning to work without saying a word to anyone other than the person on the phone. Unlike Tatum, she had missed an opportunity to make a brief connection with a friendly man who would have added a bit of joy to her evening by simply being his happy-go-lucky self.

Tatum sighed as she looked over the top of the bag of food she had set on the counter and watched her mom return to her office. It was a reminder of everything wrong in the Snyder household but she didn't know what she could do to fix any of it. So, having allowed her mother to quickly but unwittingly zap her own bit of newfound happiness, she swallowed her disappointment and began to unload the white take-out boxes with the red dragons on the front.

The food looked and smelled delicious. Interestingly enough, it was being shared "family style" but, certainly not with any sense of togetherness. She filled two plates with food, one for herself and one for Kinsey. She chose nearly equal portions but gave Kinsey a little extra fried rice because she knew he liked it better than the Kung Pao San Yan.

Tatum took the plates upstairs and knocked on Kinsey's bedroom door as Grant went into the kitchen to prepare a plate for himself. Kinsey's room was very neatly organized, a lot like his mother's home office. They likely shared this trait because they both spent as much time in their own spaces as they could.

"Dinner," Tatum said through the door.

"Come in," Kinsey responded as he set his geography textbook down. "Thanks," he added as the door opened and he stood up to take the plate. "What'd we get?" After a brief inspection, "Oh, Happy Feast. Looks good."

"Doing your homework?" Tatum asked.

"Yep," Kinsey replied. "States and capitals. You?"

"Yeah," Tatum sighed in preparation to add a hint of sarcasm. "I'm doing grammar. Awesome. Enjoy your dinner. I'll be in to quiz you in about an hour or so, okay?"

"Thanks," Kinsey said after they nodded in agreement and before watching his sister leave. He returned to his spot, sat back down in front of his book, and dug into his food.

Tatum took her plate to her messy room and was about to try and clear a space on the desk where she could set her dinner. After a bit of head-swiveling inspection, she ultimately decided to set her plate on a closed Washington State History textbook because there just wasn't enough desk space for everything and she didn't want to take the time to clean and organize while risking her food getting cold. Even though they enjoyed each other, she and her brother did their homework and ate their dinners separately at opposite ends of the hallway in their own, very dissimilar rooms.

Downstairs, Grant had loaded up his plate and grabbed a second beer from the refrigerator before walking to the family room to plop down on the couch and watch the season opening University of Washington Huskies basketball game against St.

Martin's. The irony of spending most of his evenings alone in a room named for family involvement was not lost on him. Tonight, when he first got home, he had a brief conversation with Tatum about what to expect for dinner sprinkled with a couple of pleasantries about the day they had each had. Otherwise, he hadn't seen or talked to anyone else in the family the entire night. And, now, he was eating his *family style* dinner in the *family room* - alone and, except for the television, in complete silence. Little did he realize that, that was about to drastically change.

On the opposite side of the house, Jill continued working in her office for another half hour. She had emails to answer from sellers, potential buyers and the higher ups at the main office. She also had fliers to organize and send to the printer for houses that had been on the market for a while and were either running out of existing fliers or had been forced to slash their asking prices. In addition, she had just received two new listings, which of course, would also require fliers. The latter would take the most time since she had to organize pictures and write text to plug into one of her templates.

Finally, she reached a good stopping point and headed into the kitchen to fill her plate. She took what was left of the barely warm Chinese food, zapped it in the microwave for about a minute and a half, and marched it back to her office to continue working. It wasn't much of a break but it was all she felt she could allow herself.

This had become the standard routine around the Snyder household. So, there they were, eating their dinners separately in the four corners of the house. Not one of them had any idea how much they would eventually regret these wasted nights. Unbeknownst to them, the catalyst for that regret was quickly getting closer. The separation they now voluntarily chose for themselves would soon be amplified and forced upon them with an intensity that they could not begin to imagine.

CHAPTER EIGHT
Billowing

Jill left her office and hustled toward the kitchen. She was carrying her dirty plate and silverware, which now contained only the saucy remnants of dinner, and an empty water glass that she was planning to refill. She entered the kitchen and placed the dirty dishes in the nearly full sink. When she turned to approach the refrigerator, she noticed that the refrigerator door was just barely open and she knew exactly who was at fault because this was a repeated infraction. The compounded frustrations from all of the previous events, coupled with irritations from much bigger problems in her marriage relationship, all boiled back to the surface and she instantly became hot-tempered. Setting her glass down on the counter hard enough to release a hint of rage but not hard enough to break it, her blood pressure rose quickly as she stared at the ever so slightly ajar refrigerator door.

"Grant!" she yelled.

Grant sat in the family room, having moved only a few times either to get more beer or to use the restroom. The sound of his wife's voice was a shrill reminder that he was not in a place of solace. He thought briefly before responding and realized that he must not have fully closed the refrigerator door when he grabbed his last beer. This was a long-standing pet peeve of Jill's. If he had to guess, he would probably estimate the argument that was coming was approximately the 200th that had started over this very thing. However, they both knew that the refrigerator door had very little to do with what they were really fighting about. Tonight, the fight would quickly evolve and the true underlying cause of their anger would, as it eventually always does, rear its ugly head.

"Yeah," Grant yelled back, feigning innocence.

"You know how I knew you were home?" she asked.

"The sound of the basketball game on the TV?" Grant suggested with no real hope of being accurate. Also knowing all too well she didn't have any deep concerns over what the score of the game was, he decided to update her anyway. "Huskies are up by eight about twelve minutes into the second half, by the way."

"Good for them!" she drowned in sarcasm as she shouted back with venom in her voice before continuing to press on the matter she actually wanted to discuss. "I knew you were home because of the open refrigerator door!"

"Oh," he said as if he hadn't already guessed that was exactly what she was going to say. "Sorry. Must've hurried out of there because of the game and forgot. Won't happen again."

"I've heard that before," Jill barked, unable to let it go. "Probably a thousand times."

"I know," Grant sincerely admitted. "I'm sorry."

"Sure you are."

Her persistence infuriated Grant, causing him to slam his beer on the coffee table. "I said I was sorry!" he shouted, no longer making any attempt to hide his feelings. "What more do you want from me?"

"I want you to stop doing it!" she yelled back, completely incensed.

Grant stood up, ready for battle. He stormed toward the kitchen as he yelled, "You know what I want? I want my wife back! The only way I knew you were home was because I saw your car. I haven't seen you all night." Grant finally entered the kitchen. "Oh, there she is. I'd practically forgotten what she looked like. Kind of pretty if you can see past the scowl."

~

Upstairs, both Kinsey and Tatum had started listening to the fight from inside their rooms. They each opened their door and poked their head out. They looked toward the noise and slumped to the floor in unison. Then, sensing each other, they looked despondently toward one another.

"Game on," Kinsey said.

"Yep," Tatum agreed.

~

Marriage takes effort to work properly. All relationships do. Jill and Grant were both hard working people when it came to their jobs but neither of them had put any real effort into their marriage in a long time.

If you think of a relationship like a bank account, Jill and Grant made a lot of deposits and few withdrawals in the beginning because they were in love. As time went on, however, the deposits slowed down and the withdrawals remained steady. Unfortunately, this is a common pattern in many relationships.

When Jill went back to work and Grant became bitter about it, the deposits from both of them stopped completely but the withdrawals never did. In fact, lately, the withdrawals had increased exponentially. As a result, the account was essentially empty. This was the night it would finally be overdrawn.

"Don't you make this about something it's not," Jill shouted. "You always do that. You always try to turn the tables. I didn't leave the refrigerator door open. You did!"

"Does that make what I said any less true?" Grant countered. Waiting for a response that was clearly never coming, he decided to ask again. "Well... Does it?"

"You're avoiding your fault in this," Jill demanded.

"Fault in what?" Grant asked. "The refrigerator? I already said I was sorry. I did it. I admitted to it. I apologized. Twice, actually. I even said I wouldn't do it again. How is that avoiding my fault in the situation? It's not, is it? The only person here avoiding anything is you. You're avoiding the whole family!"

"And you're not?" Jill asked. "What do you call eating dinner and drinking beer alone in front of the TV every night?"

"Relaxing," Grant fired back. "Anyone who wants to join me is more than welcome. What do you call hiding out in your office with the door closed? An invitation?"

"I have work to do."

"Whatever helps you sleep at night," Grant said, sarcastically. "Isn't that what the beer's for?"

"God knows I need something to knock me out in the middle of all your snoring."

"I don't snore," Jill shielded.

"The heck you don't, Chewbacca," Grant sneered. "Just go

hole up in your sanctuary already."

"Where else would I want to be?"

"Obviously not here."

"You've got that right," Jill blasted back.

"What do you know?" Grant observed. "We actually agree on something. I can't remember the last time that happened. Can you?"

"Why don't you just get it over with?" Jill scorned. "Divorce me already!"

~

Tatum and Kinsey shared a look of complete dismay that nearly stated *Here it is* without using any words. Their worst fears seemed to be on the verge of coming true. However, at that instant, neither of them could possibly know just how long it would be before they would be able to look each other directly in the eyes again.

~

After a brief moment of silence, in which Grant's heart hardened nearly beyond repair, he responded, "You've got it."

~

And, there it was.

For Tatum, it was as though someone had poured liquid lead into her heart. The weight of sorrow is incalculable but, if it could be measured, it might be the heaviest substance on earth.

Kinsey, on the other hand, had been bottling his sorrow for far too long. He couldn't contain it any longer. His emotional bubble had irreversibly burst and the moment for him to explode had finally arrived.

CHAPTER NINE
The First to Go

Without any kind of warning, physical or verbal, Kinsey leapt to his feet and started sprinting. As years worth of pent-up tension and anxiety were unleashed in an outpouring of turbulent rage, he bolted from his bedroom doorway and sprinted down the hall, took a hard left at the staircase, and bounded down the flight of stairs, quickly reaching the front door. He forcefully swung the door open and continued his hasty escape. The emotive time bomb within Kinsey Snyder had officially been detonated.

Tatum watched, shocked and unsure of how, or even if, she should respond. It appeared that, for the first time in her recent memory, Kinsey was doing something with great focus and purpose. But, what was it and why? It was clearly connected to the fight between their parents, but that is where the clarity ended. Already in a heightened emotional state herself, also quite clearly because of the raging fight going on downstairs and the "D" word being added to the mix, Tatum felt an expansion of negative feelings rising inside of her. It was as though her emotional immune system had finally been cracked open and Kinsey's flare-up was extremely contagious. The whole Snyder family was being infected and they didn't even realize it.

With Kinsey already outside, Tatum began silently trembling, as if there really was no reaction that could properly demonstrate the severity of what was happening all around her, until she finally and simply muttered, "Kinsey?"

She got to her feet and walked, slowly at first but with steadily increasing speed, and started wandering down the stairs and toward the doorway. Tatum was no longer paying attention to the fight between her parents. The fact that the intensity of their screaming had actually increased didn't even register with her because Kinsey's perplexing reaction had captured her total concentration and undivided attention.

When she reached the open door, she saw Kinsey still sprinting away from the house as fast as he could and heading directly toward the forest on the other side of the cul-de-sac. It sounded as though he was yelling something but she couldn't make it out no matter how hard she tried. Perhaps it wasn't actually words but more of an anguished groan from the depths of his soul.

"Kinsey," she said again but only a little louder than before.

Without another word, she suddenly started to chase after him. "Kinsey," she was ultimately able to shout, but not until she reached the edge of their yard and just before she bounded over the sidewalk and into the street. "Kinsey!"

Tatum was older but, even if she hadn't been, she was born a better athlete than Kinsey. She probably inherited it from her father. He had played a lot of different sports when he was growing up and, from what she had been told, he was pretty good at them. Of course, her mom had to be rather athletic to be a cheerleader in high school, too. Perhaps she got some of it from either side. Wherever it came from, she inherited more of it than Kinsey did and her speed enabled her to progressively gain on her brother. As she got closer to him, she could hear his screaming getting louder. Actual words were becoming clearer now.

"No more," he was repeatedly shouting. "No more!"

It didn't dawn on her until later, but this might have been the first time in years that she had heard her brother shout anything. He was a quiet kid of few words, and often even lethargic in both demeanor and speech. He even turned into a bit of a mumbler in certain settings. It mostly happened in a group of strangers or in a group that was too large for his comfort level. In those situations, he found it difficult to contain his nervousness.

No more what? Tatum wondered as she ran as hard as her body could carry her. He could have meant no more fighting. He could have meant no more neglect. He could have simply and generally meant no more of the pressure that had been pushing in on him from his exterior circumstances over the last several years. Maybe the poor kid was fed up with his entire life. *Whatever it is,* she thought, *he has clearly taken more of it than he can handle.*

This was also likely the first time Tatum had seen Kinsey exert this much energy. His lethargy wasn't laziness, it was a physical manifestation of both his unhappiness and feeling of helplessness to do anything about it. This had made him shy and somber, unwilling to participate or speak up about anything.

This complete shift in character was sudden and alarming. It was as though a dormant volcano had finally erupted and the built-up energy was scattering itself all over everything in sight. It was shocking, exciting, and terrifying all at the same time.

Tatum didn't know what to do, other than to chase him down and comfort him. She continued running after him, proud to see him finally letting his emotions out and, hoping desperately that she would catch him soon so she could hold him and promise again that nothing would ever keep them apart. Had Tatum taken the time to think back on her relationship with her brother, she wouldn't have been able to conjure up a single memory in which she had broken a promise to him. And, if she had to pick from all of the promises that she had made to Kinsey over the years, this would have been the most important.

There was no one in the world that she loved more than her little brother and she had felt that way since the day her parents gave her the good news that she was about five or six months away from becoming a big sister. Tatum never experienced the jealous feelings that many older siblings do. In fact, the months that followed her parents' announcement were excruciating with anticipation. It was like waiting for Christmas when you know what you're getting and it's the gift you want more than anything in the world. The day she met Kinsey in the hospital was just like Christmas morning. She immediately loved her little brother just as much as anyone possibly could.

Unlike a child's love affair with most individual Christmas presents, little had changed in her feelings for that gift over the nine years that followed. As they got older, the dynamic of their relationship changed some but, not the love or protective instinct that she had felt that first day. She would still do anything in her power to protect him from the horrors of the world around him, including the awful pain and dreadfulness that comes with a broken family relationship. She wasn't able to heal things between her parents who, in her opinion, seemed far more determined to punish than to love each other. But comforting Kinsey was something she could do. And, as she continued to gain on him, she had every intention of catching up and doing exactly that.

She was just about to call his name one more time when she felt a strange energy field suddenly build in front of her like a strong head wind. It momentarily slowed her run to less than half speed. Then, swiftly and unexplainably, right before her eyes, Kinsey abruptly vanished into thin air.

CHAPTER TEN
Panic

Tatum lunged forward as a severe wave of headwind force caused by the energy field in front of her reversed itself, like a leaf blower turning into a vacuum that pulled her toward the epicenter, and then rapidly disappeared with her little brother and some of the loose forest debris from the area that had surrounded him. She stopped her momentum with a tottering shuffle of her feet and stood still, staring in bewildered silence at the spot where Kinsey had just been.

Shock and confusion overwhelmed both her motionless body and her jumbled emotions. The event she had just witnessed was so baffling it took what felt like minutes to even begin to process. Anxiety finally took over and her heartbeat rapidly picked up its pace.

"Where...?" she finally inquired out loud, so flummoxed she was unable to string together a simple complete sentence. She quietly spun in circles with her eyes darting all over the forest. "What was…? What hap… Kinsey? How? But… Kinsey!"

As a tidal wave of terror washed over her, she abruptly sprinted over to the spot where the incident occurred and looked all around in frantic agitation. There was no explaining it but it had happened. It made absolutely no sense but she had felt the energy and seen the perplexing event with her very own eyes. Kinsey had suddenly and mysteriously disappeared without even the slightest trace of having been there and, even more importantly, without a clue as to where he had gone.

The thought of Kinsey's reaction being a response to his inability to handle any more of the pressures that had been pushing in on him for the last several years resurfaced in her mind. She wondered briefly if this could have had something to do with Kinsey pushing back. *Maybe that was the energy I felt*, she thought. *If that's what this was, the pressure won.*

Gloom immediately landed in her heart like a cartoon piano dropped by movers from the tenth story of an apartment building. Her gloom was quickly overtaken by her anxiety and, suddenly, the thought vanished as quickly as Kinsey had. She couldn't really hold any thought in her head at the moment. That's what true terror does to a person. It scatters the brain like a pile of leaves getting hit by a sudden and powerful gust of wind.

"Kinsey!" she kept yelling. "KINSEY!"

She looked everywhere. There was no hole that he could have fallen into. No jungle booby-trap apparatus that had lifted him into the air. He didn't appear to have gone anywhere nearby. But, there was no visible force field that could have transported him somewhere far away either. Of course there wasn't. This wasn't a Saturday morning cartoon. This was her brother in the woods by their house. But, what had happened was beyond understanding so, maybe thinking about explanations of the mystical or paranormal kind wasn't so crazy, right? After all, she had seen something she didn't understand. She had felt the pressure of whatever it was that happened. And, something definitely did happen whether the evidence of it was visible or not.

"Kinsey!" She was now screaming. "KINSEY!"

Some invisible force had just sucked her brother out of her presence and a logical explanation simply wasn't possible. But, without an explanation, there was no way to know what to do. Assuming her brother was alive, she had to know where he went in order to formulate a plan for getting him back. And, she was going to get him back alive and well. She had made a promise.

Whatever it was that had happened, and whatever was going to be done about it, Tatum wasn't going to be able to figure it out alone. After searching the area for a solid ten minutes, which felt like hours, and making absolutely no progress whatsoever, she realized she had to get her parents to help.

Tatum turned toward the house and started running again without a single thought regarding her parents' fight. She had tunnel vision. All that the human cheetah could think of at that moment was getting their help and finding Kinsey. Wherever he was, if he was alive, he must be scared out of his mind. He needed her now more than ever before and she was determined to help him no matter what it took.

The harder she ran, the greater the volume of tears that streamed down her face. This was an extraordinary situation and the combination of confusion, grief, and fear was almost too much for the normally resilient twelve year-old girl to handle. The only thing keeping her from falling apart was the exact thing that was taking her to the brink of a nervous breakdown: the mission to rescue her little brother from whatever it was that had stolen him from her company.

Tatum stormed up the same steps she had gone down less than twenty minutes earlier and hurried through the open doorway. She rushed down the hallway and toward the kitchen where her parents were still squawking at one another, but under the circumstances, she failed to even take notice of the ongoing battle.

"You've wanted this for years anyway!" Jill shouted. "You know you have!"

"And you haven't?" Grant asked.

"You bet I have," Jill responded. "If it wasn't for the kids-"

"He's gone!" Tatum shrieked as she burst into the kitchen at full speed and stopped abruptly. "Kinsey's gone!"

Both parents paused the shouting and turned to look at their daughter.

"What do you mean, gone?" Jill inquired, puzzled.

"I mean gone, gone," Tatum answered. "You have to help me find him."

"He's not in his room?" Grant asked.

"No," Tatum explained, irritated. "He ran out of the house when he heard you guys talking about getting a divorce. I promised him. I promised him that nothing would ever separate us and now…"

Grant and Jill glanced at each other with a hint of guilt before Grant interjected while already starting to head for the front door, "He's probably just in the yard. I'll talk to him."

"Dad, he's really gone," Tatum insisted. If there were ever a moment when she needed her parents to pay attention to what she was telling them, this was it. "I chased him out of the house and he ran into the woods and disappeared."

"So, he's hiding," Jill cut in.

"He's not hiding," Tatum clarified emphatically. "Listen to me for once. He literally…" While she was aware that there wasn't a way to tell her parents what she had to say without sounding totally crazy, she also knew that she didn't have time to waste and finally gave in to finish her sentence. "He literally evaporated."

CHAPTER ELEVEN
Those Who Followed

"Evaporated?" Grant asked, as if his daughter had just announced she was an alien with superpowers.

"Yes," Tatum confirmed, mournfully. The difference in emotion between Tatum and her parents was palpable. To them, her words sounded ridiculous. But, for Tatum, they were an honest plea for help with a strength that easily outweighed all of the other times in the past when she had put her head down and done what was expected of her without asking for anything in return.

"Okay," Jill said, disbelieving. "We're sorry you heard us fighting but, this behavior is absolutely unacceptable. Enough with the games already."

"Do I look like I'm playing a game?" Tatum asked, both discouraged and growing angry. "I saw something out there. I felt something out there. It wasn't visible but I know what I experienced."

"Honey," Grant started with an apologetic tone, "you understand why that sounds-"

"Yep," Tatum interrupted. "But, my little brother, the boy you two are really responsible for even though I've pretty much been raising him for the last few years, is gone, and now you're wasting time."

A wave of guilt hit that kitchen like a tsunami at the beach as Grant looked more closely at Tatum's mottled red and tear-drenched face. She looked as though she was more likely to either explode or implode than she was to remain still. He glanced at his wife, who looked as stunned as he'd ever seen her, then back to Tatum. To his knowledge, his daughter had never lied before. Not about even the most mundane thing. It was safe to assume that she was telling the truth now.

With the emerging realization that, at the very least, Tatum seemed to believe what she was saying, fear began to take hold. The culpability he was feeling would have to wait. "Take us to where this happened," Grant said. He moved toward the door and Tatum hurried to lead them outside with her mother, shell-shocked by shame whether she was ready to admit it or not, in tow.

As they stepped off the porch, Jill couldn't help but remain skeptical, "Tatum, if this turns out to be a hoax…"

"It isn't," Tatum insisted. "You don't understand. Kinsey has been bottling everything up for I don't know how long now. And, if you don't know what I'm talking about then you've been paying even less attention than I thought. He finally let it out and, when he did…"

"What?" Jill asked with a hint of increasing sarcasm. "When he did, what? The outcry over how horrible his parents are was too much for the universe to handle and he spontaneously evaporated?"

"I don't know what happened."

"Well, he didn't evaporate. That much you can absolutely, positively be sure of."

"I wish I was."

"Come on, honey. We haven't been perfect but you're laying it on a little thick right now, aren't you?"

"You don't get it so, I'm obviously not laying it on thick enough. Just follow me." She continued to lead her parents toward the spot where she had seen Kinsey vanish, jogging as swiftly as her parents could manage.

As they got closer and the spot came into view, Jill noticed that her daughter's lower lip began to quiver. She looked sad and scared. Jill finally began to realize that this might not be a game at all and she felt ashamed as the fear that had taken root in Grant began to spread to his wife.

"There it is," Tatum said as she pointed at the spot.

"Right there?" Grant asked, baffled. "But, there's nothing really there."

"Exactly," Tatum agreed.

"Tell us precisely what happened," Jill said with authentic belief in her suddenly unnerved voice.

"He kept running," Tatum described. "He kept running and yelling. 'No more! No more!' I was chasing him and all of a sudden he was gone. He was just gone."

"That doesn't make any sense at all," Grant persisted. "Your mom is right. People don't just evaporate."

"Kinsey did," Tatum said, no longer able to hold back the tears. "I felt the pressure of the energy on the front of my body and then it went the other way and pulled me toward where he had been but, by then, he was already gone."

"Oh, my," Jill gasped as the reality of what was happening truly set in. She started to go to pieces and search frantically. "Kinsey. Kinsey! KINSEY!"

"Don't panic," Grant said, attempting to calm his wife.

"Don't panic?!" Jill roared as she let loose with a string of hysterical punches to Grant's chest. "My son is missing!"

"We'll find him," Grant said as he tried to pull Jill in and comfort her.

"Then start looking!" she shouted as she pulled away from him and went back to searching for her son. "Kinsey! Kinsey! Where are you? Kinsey!"

Grant was used to his wife directing her anger toward him. But, it had been a while since he had seen her express this much concern for the members of their family. He knew that concern was there, even if he wouldn't admit that to her, and he had longed to get her to show it to them. Unfortunately, he hadn't seen it in a very long time. Had he not been so worried about Kinsey, he may have taken a moment to appreciate it.

Instead, Grant started searching the forest as intently as Jill and Tatum. If Kinsey had simply wanted their attention, he had certainly gotten it.

Although she couldn't know it, the passion and intensity that overwhelmed Jill at that moment, was exactly the same type of emotion as her son had been feeling when he disappeared. And, accordingly, as she reached the same spot where Kinsey was last seen, she began to feel the increasing pressure of an energy field for the first time.

Rather than pressing in on her the way it had on Tatum when Kinsey disappeared, however, this energy felt as though it was gushing out of her from every pore of her skin until, just when she thought she was about to explode, everything went dark for her and she simply vanished as well.

Neither Grant nor Tatum saw it happen but the feeling of a swirling wind that hit them in their backs and then their faces, coupled with the sudden silence from Jill's missing shouts, caused them to look toward where they thought they knew Jill to be.

"Jill?" Grant said, suddenly frenzied.

"Mom?" Tatum yelled. Unable to take any more trauma, she dropped to her knees in the dirt and sobbed. Tatum was the one member of the Snyder family who had truly managed to keep it together while the foundations of her family were being tattered over the last couple of years. Now, in about the same amount of time that it takes to get a pizza delivered, her incredible level of resilience had completely eroded. "What is happening to my family?"

Grant ran over to his daughter, just as mystified as she was. He was rapidly filled with overwhelming regret and suddenly became aware of an increasing flow of energy escaping from his body, springing from the inside out. "I don't know sweetie," he whispered as he cradled her. And, in an instant, they too were both gone.

PART THREE
The Awakening

CHAPTER TWELVE
Alone

As he gradually regained consciousness, Kinsey felt as though he'd been in a very deep sleep for days. He was as groggy as he had ever been and his entire body felt heavy when he tried to move. He was also a bit disoriented but, his brain slowly began to return to a state of awareness and he suddenly wondered why his bed felt so hard. It reminded him of a night when he got scared during a thunder and lightning storm and slept on the floor next to his sister's bed. *She stayed awake and talked to me until I fell asleep,* he remembered fondly until his mind shifted back to his current circumstances.

Where is my pillow, he wondered. As his thoughts continued to get ahead of the rest of his body waking up, he realized that he didn't even remember falling asleep. *What is this powdery stuff in my hands,* he added to his mental list of non-verbalized questions. *Is that dirt?*

His eyes slowly opened, taking a few seconds to find their focus, and he began to realize that he wasn't in his bedroom. He wasn't even in his house…or any house for that matter. Kinsey was outside lying in the dirt. *Did I get knocked out by something,* he wondered as the number of questions continued to add up and he began a deeper search of his memory vault.

The last thing he remembered was running through the forest by his house so, the fact that he was outside and on the ground both began to make some sense. However, as Kinsey sat up and took in the forested terrain surrounding him, he came to the terrifying realization that this was not the forest he knew. This place was completely unfamiliar to him.

~

Staring at the vast, turquoise blue ocean and the wide stretch of gorgeous, white sandy beach in front of her, Tatum was totally confused. *Where am I,* she asked herself, purposely avoiding the thought that the paradise she found herself in could possibly mean she'd crossed over into the afterlife. *And, where is my dad?*

The last thing she could recall was her dad holding her in his arms. In that moment, she and her father had both been completely heartbroken with a terrifying feeling of grief but she had somehow felt safer than she did right now. Then that sensation took over her entire body. It was as if something inside her was bursting out from inside every square inch of her frame. Such a sensation would logically be painful but, in this case, it was just the opposite. The uproar of it all was simultaneously amazing and frightening, which made the experience quite thrilling.

Tatum couldn't figure out how she had gotten from where she was in the forest near their house to this strange but beautiful place. If she was dead, how did she die? *Is that what that exploding feeling was,* she wondered. *Couldn't be. Mom and Kinsey both disappeared. I have to assume I did, too. When people die, their bodies are left behind. This is something different.* But, that potential answer only raised more questions. For example, if she was simply moved somewhere, what had transported her and where had it transported her to? The whole thing was just plain confusing.

Even worse, though, was the realization that, in all likelihood, all four members of the Snyder family had now disappeared from the home they knew. But, if that really was the case, then why weren't they all together? And, if not all of them, at least her dad? They were holding on to one another when this happened, after all. So, why was she now by herself? How could she possibly be alone?

Perhaps she wasn't.

Just as Tatum had, Jill figured that her family should be somewhere close by. Returning to the desperate state of mind she was in just before her disappearance, she suddenly leapt to her feet, once again searching for her family. But, this time, she wasn't looking for just one family member. She was looking for all three of them.

"Tatum!" she screamed as she frantically searched the strange, tropical jungle she now found herself in. "Grant! Where did you go?"

Although she had been aware that she was in a foreign place from the time she woke up, Jill was now in a stunned state of mind and didn't notice the extremely lush vegetation or any of the brilliant colors that surrounded her. She didn't even realize that she was splashing through a small stream as she continued to yell, "Tatum! Grant! Kinsey!" For the first time in longer than she would ever admit, the one and only thing on her mind was her family.

She flung some giant, exotic looking green leaves out of her way as she climbed over a mossy, fallen tree. She hurdled herself off of it like an experienced explorer on an exciting adventure and continued running.

Maybe they're still asleep, she thought. *I need to yell as loud as I can and wake them up.*

"Grant!" she shouted again, at the top of her lungs before taking a deep breath of the pristine jungle air. At the same time, an elegant, bright blue-bodied peacock soared over her head, making no attempt to be stealth but without being seen or heard. "Tatum! Kinsey! Where are you? Grant! GRANT!"

~

"JILL!" Grant yelled as he ran quickly through the dense brush, circling around the side of a large boulder and ducking sideways under a leaning tree. Seemingly out of nowhere, his foot hit a low lying branch that caused him to trip, stumble a few times and then fall face first through a clearing and onto the ground, hitting hard with a loud thud and an "Oof!" He looked up and discovered that he had landed just inches from the edge of a cliff.

When Grant lifted himself up and looked out over the cliff, he realized that if he hadn't tripped on that branch he would be dead right now. In front of him was a straight drop off with a rocky bottom several hundred feet below. *Where am I?* he wondered for the second time since he had woken up. It was a question all four members of the Snyder family had asked themselves since waking up and the answer was coming, but it wouldn't bring any comfort.

Crawling backwards several feet, he sat down, pulled his knees into his chest like a frightened child and just stared at the magnificent spectacle of nature in front of him. But, instead of being awestruck by the beauty in his new mountainous surroundings, he finally began to feel the full weight of the situation he was in. He was truly scared for the first time he could remember. Not only was he alone in a strange place, but the people he cared most about must be experiencing the same thing and he couldn't do anything to help them. *We're all alone*, he thought. *All four of us. Completely alone.*

Then, suddenly, he heard the rustling of the bushes behind him and, before it had even registered in his brain, a hand touched his shoulder.

CHAPTER THIRTEEN
Strangers

The startling touch of a stranger's hand, albeit a gentle one, nearly sent Grant leaping off the cliff to his death. Instead, he bounded to his feet and spun around. Fully aware of his proximity to the edge of the cliff, he scooted forward in an athletic stance as gravel and dirt slid off and disappeared behind him. Settling into a position that kept him at the ready, he was, of course, scared but also prepared to fight whoever or whatever was attacking him. But, instead of a ferocious beast or a menacing stranger, standing in front of him was a kindly looking, portly, grey-bearded man about his father's age.

His father hadn't crossed Grant's mind much lately. Neither of his parents had. The strain in the Snyder household had caused distance in other relationships as well. Grant had always gotten along well with his parents and he still did. The distance had taken place because Grant was embarrassed by what was happening in his own home. He didn't want to admit to his parents that he wasn't having the same kind of success in his marriage that they had in theirs. And, since his father had retired and his parents had begun to travel more, it had been easy to keep their quick phone conversations more surface-level. He wasn't lying to them. Just avoiding admitting the truth. Secrets have a way of slowly causing a division in relationships, even in the rare circumstance that they manage to stay hidden.

"I'm Max," the man said as he extended a friendly hand. "Welcome."

~

"Who're you?" Jill asked, facing a stranger of her own.

"Good," the woman replied. "You speak English. This situation is even tougher and more awkward when you add a language barrier to the equation. Like I already said, I'm Elaine. Who're you?"

Jill stared at the younger woman for a moment, looking her over. She would guess the plain-looking woman to be around thirty but wondered if she wasn't older than she looked. "Jill," she finally answered. "I heard your name. I mean, where'd you come from?"

"Camp," Elaine quickly responded as if expecting the question. She nodded her head toward the hand she still had extended. "Are you going to shake this?"

"Sorry," Jill sighed as she extended a hand and shook it.

"Someone's sent to look for new arrivals every morning," Elaine began to explain, finally able to put her hand back at her side. "Most of the time there aren't any. But, we have to check every day just in case. It's a lot harder to bring people into the fold if they've been lost for a while. If they're gone too long, they usually don't last anyway. Once in a while you actually get several that arrive at the same time. It's really confusing when they show up and none of them know who the others are or how any of them, including themselves, got here. Or, where here is, for that matter. So, are you alone?"

"As far as I know," Jill replied, taking another quick glance around and hoping to somehow spot her family even though she knew in her heart they weren't there.

"Let's go," Elaine said, motioning for Jill to follow her.

"Go where?"

"Camp."

Jill's fear that Elaine's intentions might not be the most honorable, was outweighed by the more intense terror of being completely alone in this mysterious, and therefore, horrifying place. So, with trepidation, she began to follow Elaine's lead.

~

Meanwhile, Tatum found herself walking in the sand with a very pretty girl a couple of years older than her. She glanced out at the water and noticed that it was hardly moving. The slight, very gentle, glistening wrinkle of the water, made it look like turquoise blue glass being blown by a brilliant artist. She admired it briefly, even allowing a smile to begin forming. But, she abruptly stopped it. Feeling guilty for letting her mind drift from her family, her gaze returned to the unfamiliar girl by her side.

Tatum wondered if this was someone who could help her find her family, if this girl had lost anyone herself, if she had been born here, and if not, how long had she been in this place. "Moirah?" she finally inquired.

"Yeah?" Moirah responded.

Tatum took a moment, gathering courage. She had so many questions to ask, it was hard to know where to begin. She could only hope that Moirah had the answers Tatum so desperately needed. As the moment of pause ended, she decided to start at the beginning and asked, "Where are we?"

~

"None of us are exactly sure," said Ray. "We call it Kadosh. Some Jewish dude told me it means 'set apart' but I don't really know. They were calling it that long before I got here."

Kinsey took the information in, glancing at his new companion who was about the same age as he was, and then looked back down at his feet and asked another question, "Where were you before this? Where'd you come from, I mean."

"Cali," Ray answered. "Long Beach. What about you?"

"Snohomish," said Kinsey.

"Snow-what?" asked Ray.

"Snohomish," repeated Kinsey. "It's about thirty miles north of Seattle, Washington."

"Well look at us," Ray said, enthusiastically. "Two West Coasters doin' it up. I knew you were alright, Kinsey. I can read people. And, you're definitely alright."

Kinsey smiled. He was starting to trust Ray and it was nice to feel like he had a friend in this weird place they called Kadosh. Still, he couldn't help but wonder if his sister and parents were back home looking for him. He knew Tatum would be worried. He hoped his parents would be, too. Their silence over the last couple of years had allowed him a lot of time to over-think things and that had caused him to create a lot of doubts.

He doubted his physical abilities when it came to sports. He doubted his own intelligence and his capability to do well in school. He doubted his social skills and his competence when it came to making friends. But, worst of all, and this is where the other doubts all stemmed from, Kinsey doubted his parents' love for him.

~

"How long have you been here?" asked Tatum.

"I don't know exactly," Moirah answered, introspectively. "It must be a couple of years by now."

"Wow," exclaimed Tatum, already recognizing the fact that while this answered several of her questions, it also raised several more. The possibility that she could be sharing the same fate also quickly dawned on her. "So, you were about my age when you got here?"

"No," Moirah said matter-of-factly. "People don't seem to age here."

"Seriously?" asked Tatum, quickly realizing that this place was even stranger than she thought if it wasn't bound by the same rules of time as the world Tatum knew. "Huh. If my mom is here, she may not want to leave."

"Good," said Moirah. "It's easier that way."

"What's easier that way?" asked Tatum with obvious apprehension.

"Accepting the truth," answered Moirah.

"What truth?" Tatum persisted.

Moirah stopped walking and turned toward Tatum, looking her in the eyes as if both to make her point clear and to somehow share the sadness that she knew her answer would cause. "No one ever leaves."

CHAPTER FOURTEEN
Friends

Tatum stood dumbfounded, anxiety coursing through her veins like it was in a hydroplane boat racing three hundred miles per hour through the rivers of her bloodstream. The thought of never leaving this place and the possibility of never seeing her family again was unfathomable.

She and Moirah stared at one another. Neither one of them knew what to say next. In those few seconds of silence, Tatum's emotions went through several changes. It started out as fear but soon turned to anger and, ultimately, became a strong sense of determination. That determination was fully displayed on Tatum's face as she exclaimed to Moirah, "There's a first time for everything."

"I'm sorry, Tatum" Moirah responded, sadly. "But, not this."

"Everything," Tatum insisted as Moirah looked at her with

sympathy, which caused Tatum to feel like she needed to re-emphasize her point. Speaking slower and more insistently, she repeated herself, "Everything."

~

Grant and Max continued walking in silence as Grant finally began to take in the beauty of his surroundings. They were high on a mountaintop so, it seemed as though he could see forever. There were about a dozen other mountain peaks around them, separated by extensive valleys. Even the gray rocks seemed beautiful because of the way they contrasted with their surroundings, which were made up of assorted shades of brown and a wide variety of lush greens.

The most beautiful things, however, were the four majestic bald eagles that soared overhead. Their dark brown bodies, book-ended by white tails and heads with yellow feet and hooked beaks were regal in appearance. Their wings spread out to over seven feet in length as they glided effortlessly through the air. It struck him in that moment that, although he understood himself to be in a foreign place, perhaps even a foreign world, this place looked an awful lot like something close to home. *Maybe Max has it wrong,* Grant thought as he briefly looked over at his new acquaintance. Unfortunately, the fanciful idea of having been transported to another world somehow now made more sense, after what he had just experienced, than the idea of being somewhere close to home. Back home, however, he had rarely taken the time to appreciate the beauty of his surroundings. Even if he had, he wasn't sure he'd ever had the opportunity to witness something this magnificent.

As if feeling Grant's glance but not acknowledging it, Max broke the silence, "You're lucky, you know."

"Not how I would currently describe it," Grant fired back.

"What I mean is," Max explained, "I arrived in winter. Wasn't exactly dressed for it either. I showed up in Bermuda shorts and flip-flops."

Grant chuckled a bit before asking, "It gets pretty cold up here, huh?"

"You'll find out just how cold in the coming weeks," Max told him. "Wait and see. You got here just in the nick of time."

"Oh good," Grant responded sarcastically. "Something to look forward to."

~

Jill, still following Elaine through the exotic jungle, began to wonder if her family would somehow be waiting for her back at the camp that they were trekking toward. She started to allow herself to be hopeful, which felt comforting.

But, then she remembered having confirmed with Elaine that she was today's only arrival and hope turned back to sadness. She wondered where her family could possibly be. *Could there be other parts to this same world?* she thought. *Or, could they have been scattered to other, entirely different worlds?* "How many are there?" she suddenly asked, trying to put the grief out of her mind. "People, I mean. At the camp?"

"About seventy or eighty," Elaine answered.

"With that many people not going anywhere," Jill responded, "it sounds more like a village than a camp, don't you think?"

"A village," Elaine pondered out loud. "I kind of like that. I think you might be right."

~

Kinsey followed Ray across a log that had fallen from one side of the narrow river to the other and acted as a bridge. He held onto various branches that reached toward the sky to balance himself as he crossed. It was a short distance but, it still made him nervous and, he went at a cautious pace. Ray, on the other hand, walked over it quickly like it wasn't a big deal. He'd done it several times before but he was also just a naturally braver kid than Kinsey was.

"You've got it," Ray said, looking back encouragingly as he hopped off on the other side and turned the rest of his body around while he watched Kinsey moving a little slow. "Come on, buddy."

"I'm coming," Kinsey said, taking the last few steps before he finally reached the other side and stepped off of the log to follow his new friend up a steep hill.

"We're almost there," Ray announced.

"It's quite a hike," Kinsey added.

"Tell me about it," Ray agreed. "This is my third trip. You'll have to make it again at some point, too. We all take turns finding the new arrivals. The first couple of times you go back with a partner to make sure you know the way. This is my second trip by myself. Maybe I'll go with you next time."

Kinsey secretly hoped that would never happen. He wanted to find a way home before his turn came. Regardless of any doubts he had about his parents' love for him, home was better than this unfamiliar place. At least at home he had Tatum. But, he decided not to say anything to Ray about that for now. Instead, he changed the subject, "Almost there, you said?"

"Yep," Ray responded. "It's just on the other side of this next hill."

"Good," said Kinsey, sincerely. But when he reached the peak of the hill they were on, he realized that the next hill was more of a mini-mountain. "Oh, just on the other side of the next hill, huh?" he said sarcastically. Kinsey already found it easy to open up and show some personality with Ray, which surprised him under the circumstances. "That's great news, Ray. It really is. By the time we get there, someone else will probably be on their way out here to greet the next round of new arrivals."

"Probably," Ray responded with a laugh. "You're alright, Kinsey."

~

Tatum and Moirah were climbing up a large rock formation that jetted out into the ocean, separating two beautiful beaches, when a logical question popped into Tatum's mind. She immediately asked, "Why not just move the camp to the place where the new arrivals show up? Then no one would have to make this trek anymore."

"Apparently," Moirah answered, "that's the way it was at first but, as more people come, more space is needed so, they've had to move the camp to different parts of the island a number of times. We moved to the camp we're going to now about a year ago. So, it's the second home I've known in Kadosh."

"This is an island?" Tatum asked, backing the conversation up a couple of sentences.

"Yep," Moirah confirmed. "Pretty big one."

Moirah reached the top of the formation and spun around, bending over and reaching a hand down to help Tatum up. The team effort was quickly successful and when Tatum got to her feet, they both turned around and looked down at the camp as Moirah said, "And, there you have it. Home, sweet home."

CHAPTER FIFTEEN
A New Kind of Family

Grant and Max finally reached the valley and approached the campsite. Stopping for a moment to scan what he was trying to accept as his new dwelling, Grant felt like he had traveled back in time. It was like a village right out of the middle ages or a movie set for a film about King Arthur or Robin Hood.

For a split second, Grant forgot where he was and let his mind flash back on the different Robin Hood movies he had seen. It started with the animated 1973 Disney version where Robin Hood and Maid Marian were both foxes and Friar Tuck was a bear. He had loved that movie when he was a kid and introduced his own children to it years ago.

He also liked the Kevin Costner version that came out in 1991. It didn't bother him that Costner's English accent went in and out and he thought it was silly that people focused in on that and made such a big deal out of it. He enjoyed the new take on the classic story and the Bryan Adams song that went along with it, even though he had gotten sick of the song at the time because the radio stations had overplayed it.

Grant didn't care for Mel Brooks' satire version, *Men in Tights,* but that was more because he always found Mel Brooks' sense of humor a little too silly and over-the-top. He did, however, thoroughly enjoy the very serious Ridley Scott version that came out in 2010 with Russell Crowe playing the lead role. He wished it had been more well received because it would have set up a fascinating franchise of sequels had it done well enough to continue. There were, of course, many other versions starring the likes of Sean Connery and Errol Flynn but Grant had never seen any of those.

The next thing Grant noticed, as his mind snapped back to the present, was that the people in the camp were all men. When this realization hit, it took him aback more than anything that had preceded it. As the community began to wave and check him out as well, Grant turned to Max, confused, and inquired, "Where are the women and children?"

~

"The rumor is," Ray explained to Kinsey, "that the men are

on the North island, the women are on the South island, the girls are on the West island, and we're on the East island."

Kinsey pondered this as he stared at an all-boy community living and working in what appeared to be an intricate set-up of tree-forts. "So, the rest of our families are here?"

"We don't know that," Ray responded. We just have rumors that men, women, boys and girls have been divided up onto different islands. There's no way of knowing for sure if that's even true or not. And, even if it is, we couldn't possibly know the specifics of who is and who isn't on those other islands."

"Of course," Kinsey agreed. Thinking a moment and trying to move on to what they did know, he finally asked, "How'd we get separated?"

"How'd we get here in the first place?" Ray fired back with a shrug of his shoulders. "That's the million dollar question."

~

"How do we get to the other islands?" Jill asked as she finally turned away from the village full of jungle huts to look Elaine in the eyes.

"We don't," Elaine said matter-of-factly.

"That's unacceptable," Jill snapped. "My family is out there and I-"

"You don't know that," Elaine insisted, interrupting. "None of us do. This, right here, is how it has always been... and it always will be."

"I won't accept that. Things change."

"Some things maybe," Elaine replied. "Not this. No way."

~

"Supposedly, some girls tried to venture off the island a long time ago," Moirah rationalized when Tatum suggested visiting the other islands.

"What happened?" asked Tatum. She looked back at the camp in front of her full of make-shift homes made from bamboo that reminded her of an old British movie from the late nineteen forties called 'The Blue Lagoon' that she had seen a rerun of on a television cable channel a couple of years earlier.

"There is a fifth island in the middle of all the others," Moirah clarified, "inhabited by the god of this world: Raum. And, let's just say, Raum likes things left the way they are. And, we like to keep Raum from getting angry. So, let's put this conversation to rest. Come on, let me introduce you to the others."

~

Kinsey was timid as Ray introduced him to the other boys, which was in stark contrast to Ray's gregarious nature. Ray seemed to have a personal connection with everyone he came into contact with and it managed to put Kinsey at ease, making him feel instantly part of the group because Ray was the one bringing him in. It allowed Kinsey to be friendlier with his new acquaintances than he otherwise would have been.

As they made the rounds, Kinsey quickly discovered that the boys were very organized and he assumed that it must have taken a great deal of time to make it that way. Each boy had a purpose, a job. There were hunters, cooks, tailors, builders, and even guards that took shifts to watch for predators that might threaten the camp. Although Ray tried to brush it off when Kinsey inquired about the types of predators that may be out there, the unwillingness to explain and clear desire to quickly move on from the subject left Kinsey quite curious and, understandably, more than a little fearful.

Kinsey began to wonder what his job would be. He couldn't think of any skills that he had that would be particularly useful in such a primitive setting. Nothing about mediocre school grades seemed to directly translate.

Then it dawned on him that he had a knack for video games that involved shooting things. But, he had never actually killed a living creature and wondered if, when the opportunity presented itself, he would actually be capable of doing so. Plus, it was fairly safe to assume that the boys had not managed to build any kind of a gun. They were probably hunting with spears or something and that was an entirely different undertaking.

Ray's job was serving as one of the counselors to the leader of the group, a 17 year-old named Trevor, who seemed friendly enough. Being a counselor basically meant that Ray conveyed the opinions of the community to Trevor who took that information and made decisions. Not that there were typically all that many decisions to be made. Things apparently ran fairly smoothly most of the time and the big decisions that got things organized to begin with were made long before Trevor had even arrived.

Little did Trevor know, however, that the arrival of Kinsey Snyder, who seemed deceitfully unassuming and harmless enough, would soon create quite a stir that would force them to finally face an issue Trevor and the rest of the community had, so far, always managed to avoid. And, Trevor would quickly wish that the subject had been left alone.

CHAPTER SIXTEEN
Remembering

Tatum sat on a large piece of dried out driftwood in the area apparently used for meals and, she assumed, for community gatherings of all kinds. The driftwood made for a firm seat that felt hard against the backside of her bony frame. However, she didn't realize that she wouldn't be sitting on it long enough to cause any real discomfort.

While she was thankful that Moirah and the other girls had invited her to join them for lunch, Tatum hadn't quite managed to work up an appetite yet. Therefore, the few sips she'd already taken were likely the only ones she would attempt to get down. It wasn't that the food was bad, although she certainly would never have chosen vegetable stew made with seawater for broth at home. It was more the fact that her reaction to felt stress and nerves typically manifested itself in her stomach. Her mother once explained that it was a condition that ran rampant on the female side of their family. Especially at this moment, it was not a legacy Tatum was thrilled to have inherited. Today was more stressful and nerve-racking than any day she could remember. So, it was no surprise that her stomach was upset and she simply couldn't fathom the idea of eating anything.

Instead, she sat back and tried to study the group. She wondered where everyone came from and what each person had been like before they arrived in this place. She wondered how each of them had reacted when they first got to Kadosh and how they had changed since their arrival. She was also curious as to how long each of them had been trapped here and whether or not any of them could possibly want to go home half as bad as she did. Then Tatum began to wonder where her real family was and what they were doing. She considered the possibility of all four of them being in this strange world, separated onto four of the five islands. Suddenly, she was overcome with deep sadness and felt as though she might, at any moment, throw up.

~

Elaine held Jill's hair back for her as the vomiting subsided. "It's okay," she assured her. "It actually wouldn't be normal if you didn't react like this on your first day. Just let it out. You'll be fine."

"Thanks," Jill said, beginning to feel beads of sweat forming above her eyebrows from her body working so hard. She opened her eyes for just a moment and couldn't help but remember that the chunky mess in front of her was once appetizing Chinese food. The name of one of her family's favorite restaurants, "Happy Feast," seemed a bit like a mean joke now. She closed her eyes again, trying but failing miserably, to put it all out of her mind.

That delicious food was something they had all enjoyed, something they could all agree on. Especially those cream cheese crab fried wontons. The entire family loved those and yet, even though she typically ate last, there was always one waiting for her when she finally prepared her plate. *That was nice of them*, she realized, perhaps for the first time. *Even Grant. And how did I repay them?* The guilt train is a rough way to travel and Jill couldn't visualize any upcoming opportunities that would allow her to disembark.

Then she remembered the refrigerator issue and briefly wondered if she had closed the door that Grant had left open. Not that it really mattered now. *What a silly thought*, she digressed. *What a silly thing to fight about. Of course, now that I think about it, what was the last fight we had that wasn't silly — no matter how important it seemed at the time?*

Without any warning, nausea went off like a string of firecrackers in the pit of her stomach and acid surged upward in her torso as her body forced her mouth open for the expulsion of any remaining stomach contents.

~

Kinsey sat on a log in an area quite similar to the one his sister was sitting in; however, food was a comfort to Kinsey and he was eating. Back home, Kinsey's favorite comfort food was something that Tatum made for him after school once in a while. She used flour tortillas, smothered them in butter, sprinkled them with cinnamon and sugar, baked them in the oven for a few minutes, rolled them up and handed them over as a delicious treat. Kinsey's taste buds melted like the butter inside of them every single time. Those simple little indulgences were a small slice of heaven as far as Kinsey was concerned. Unfortunately, Kinsey had to start facing the fact that delicacies as fantastic as those were, were a long way off and might never be experienced again.

Instead he, and the other boys in his group, dined on cooked rabbit. Kinsey was surprised at how moist and tender the meat was. Without any real seasonings or anything, the flavor was quite mild, but it was remarkably delicious and Kinsey was delighted to find a food he considered enjoyable in this place. Of course, in his current predicament and with food always a comfort to him, anything that wasn't completely disgusting would have been a nice surprise.

Other than the occasional chips, candy bars or the cinnamon roll tortillas his sister made for him, it was rare that Kinsey ate food that wasn't prepared in a restaurant kitchen and delivered by some stranger. Although he was, at that moment, surrounded by strangers and he was afraid to take a bite just moments earlier, he was actually enjoying it now.

~

Grant was less enthusiastic about his meal but liked the campfire atmosphere. He would have enjoyed it even more, though, had he been seated next to a cooler full of ice-cold beers and the people he was surrounded by had been his family, including Jill.

The hardened heart he felt just hours ago, filled with anger and bitterness, was already softening. Regret was beginning to set in. He knew he could have handled things with his wife a lot better. He could have been more understanding. He could have talked to her instead of sulking. He could have, but he didn't.

They used to talk. They used to talk a lot, actually. Grant remembered phone calls that lasted for hours when they were dating. He remembered Jill getting in trouble for talking to him on the phone after her ten o'clock "phone curfew" and the two of them even falling asleep on the phone because they talked until the early morning hours. Those were great memories of a time when they couldn't seem to hear each other's voices enough. *Why is it so hard to talk to each other now?* he wondered.

Absence truly does make the heart grow fonder. They hadn't been separated long but what amplified things to an unbearable degree was the fact that, from what he was hearing, it appeared likely that the absence of his family could very well be eternal.

CHAPTER SEVENTEEN
Uprising

Kinsey missed his family but, he also knew he could fit in here. In fact, he figured he could fit in a whole lot better than he did at school back home. He was never really comfortable participating in class or in any group settings for that matter. Yet, here he found himself about to ask his first question in a group larger than any class he'd ever had.

"Why do you think this Raum guy wants us separated like this?" he asked loud enough for most people to hear over the light chatter of conversations around the group. He was quickly taken aback by how silent everything suddenly became and by the fact that everyone turned to look at the new guy who had dared to pose this crazy question. He then watched every set of eyes shift over to Trevor as they waited for the answer.

"It doesn't matter why," Trevor replied stiffly. "What

matters is that we think it's for the best."

"How?" Kinsey inquired, genuinely confused.

"When we were all together, back in the world that we each came from, our lives were full of fighting and anger. We're better off this way."

"So, there's no fighting or anger here?" Kinsey inquired.

The others looked as though they were watching a tennis match, with eyes darting back and forth as they watched the dialogue between Kinsey and Trevor.

"Less," Trevor shot back. "Much less. We work together better this way. We're friends."

"And that's enough reason to stop trusting our sisters, moms and dads?" Kinsey replied. "We're supposed to just forget about them?"

"We don't have a choice," Trevor said, beginning to shift uncomfortably in his posture. "Raum wants it this way so this is the way it will stay."

"That right there raises a lot more questions," Kinsey fired back, gaining a confidence and momentum like he'd never felt before.

"Well," Trevor said, nervously, "keep them to yourself. Look, we all have a lot of questions when we first arrive. Most of us learn to accept things the way they are."

"What about those who don't?" Kinsey injected.

"Just be sure that you do. You don't want to be on your own here."

"I can't be the only one who feels this way," Kinsey stated as he looked around the group but got little response.

"The last time anyone journeyed out," Trevor sighed, "they were attacked by… They didn't make it."

"Why?" Kinsey asked. "What att-"

"Raum stopped them," Trevor stated emphatically, cutting Kinsey off. "Do you feel like dying today, new guy? None of us do. So, get those thoughts out of your head right now. Everyone just go back to eating."

The entire group, including Kinsey who showed his reluctance, did as they were told.

~

Feeling a little stronger, Tatum had grown inquisitive as well. "Is Raum the one who brought us here?"

"That's the rumor," Moirah answered, glancing around nervously as if the camp was bugged with listening devices.

"Why?"

"Why what?"

"Why would he bring us here?"

"They say he wants us cut off from the people we love."

"Mission accomplished," Tatum admitted. "How does he do it?"

Still nervous, Moirah glanced around and spoke cautiously. "The going theory is, back home, we were growing apart from our loved ones anyway and the peak of that negative energy gave Raum the power to finish the job. So, if it's true, we kind of did this to ourselves. Pathetic, huh?"

"Yeah," Tatum admitted as she looked at the ground and soaked this in for a moment. "I guess so."

It fit perfectly with the events that had happened to her. Her family was growing apart and when Kinsey finally erupted, that's when it happened. Raum was able to open some kind of doorway and pull them all through, taking them away from the world they knew. The world wherein they had allowed pieces of hell to creep into their lives. He had pulled them out of it and into this atrocious, more permanent hell they now found themselves trapped in.

Tatum let her frustrations build for a moment then looked up and fired off a statement of aggravation at Moirah: "I've always believed God loves us. And, therefore, I believe He must want us to love each other. You all call Raum the god of this world but, he sounds more like a demon to me."

"Whatever he is," Moirah responded, "you don't want to mess with him.

~

Jill stared back at Elaine with a righteous fire rising up in her eyes. "It's becoming clear to me that the longer you stay in this place, the more complacent you become, and I have no room for complacency."

~

After lunch, Grant was put through a series of aptitude tests. It was quickly determined that as a cook, he could potentially kill the entire camp. He was pretty good with his hands but, not in all areas. He showed potential as a builder, but he couldn't sew to save his life. He was a very physical person, so he might make a good guard or a hunter.

As some of the other men went to fetch weapons to test him with, Grant's mind drifted back to the very first fight he and Jill had. It happened back in high school. Grant had refused to dance at the prom. He said that people looked stupid when they danced. Jill said she didn't care. Everyone else was dancing and she wanted to do it, too. She said it wasn't about looking cool; it was about having fun. She also told him that anyone who thought he was too cool to have fun wasn't nearly as cool as he thought he was and that maybe he was the stupid one.

He chuckled a bit to himself, remembering how upset she had gotten. He liked her fiery spirit. It was part of what made him fall in love with her in the first place.

They had screamed and yelled at one another and, for the first time in any relationship he'd ever had with a girl, he was the one who backed down. Moments after fighting like two people who couldn't stand one another, they danced. She was right, too. They had so much fun that he forgot about what an idiot he probably looked like. Instead, he focused on her. After that night, he couldn't imagine life without her.

Yet, here he was in this strange place without his Jill. Instead, in her place were only regrets from the past few years where he had allowed things to get so screwed up that they had stopped talking – except to fight.

Grant turned his attention to the men around him as those bringing the weapons returned. Instead of grabbing a bow and arrow or a spear, he waved them away and began to address the crowd.

"Think back," Grant pleaded with them. "Remember your families. Your women. Your children. I happen to love mine. Something tells me each and every one of you loves yours, too. I'm not afraid of anyone or anything save one. I'm terrified of never seeing my family again. I won't let it happen and you shouldn't either. This Raum be damned!"

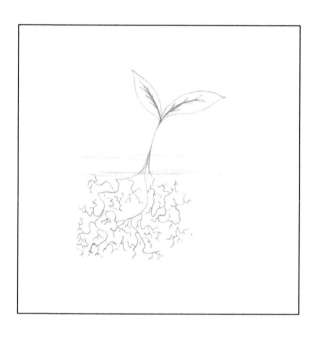

PART FOUR
A New Beginning

CHAPTER EIGHTEEN
A New Kind of Family

Inside a hut with three other women, Jill was lying in a hammock. She was the only one who was not sleeping. She scanned her surroundings and almost chuckled to herself as she thought of that old TV show from the mid 1960's, *Gilligan's Island*. Never, even on her most creative, fantasy-driven day, would she have imagined that there would be a time in her life where she would travel to a strange world and re-live a bizarre, all-women, version of that show. *Too bad the professor isn't here to help us figure out a way home,* she thought. *Of course, he didn't exactly have a lot of success getting those castaways off of their island. On second thought, maybe we're better off after all.*

Her mind began to drift to Tatum, who loved the re-runs of that show when she was a bit younger. Jill started thinking about all of the things she loved about her daughter. What a remarkable little girl she had. She was a disciplined, reliable, tenacious twelve year-old.

Suddenly, her mind took her all the way back to the day she told Grant they were going to be parents. She had broken the news over homemade pizza with green olives and pineapple in their tiny apartment. She managed a smile and almost laughed out loud as she thought about how Grant had nearly choked on a slice when she blurted out the announcement with no warning at all.

Could that really have been thirteen years ago? She wondered. *We were so happy then. We were terrified, but we were excited about both Tatum and each other. Why didn't it stay that way?*

She turned over and tried to will herself to sleep but failed. Regret was keeping her mind too active. It was clearly going to be a long night.

~

Meanwhile, Grant was suffering a similar fate. He was lying awake on something that resembled a pallet and was just as uncomfortable as it looked. He was also focused on Jill and Tatum. However, his mind had not drifted quite as far back in time. He was thinking about the night he rushed Jill to the hospital to deliver their first child.

It was not as chaotic as it was typically portrayed in movies. There was no comical moment of forgetting the overnight bag, no fainting, and Jill never punched him or screamed any obscenities.

He broke from his reverie for a moment and thought *I had never seen Jill so scared. And, quite possibly, I never will.*

Attempting to break through the sadness by letting his mind drift back again, he recalled that every ounce of fear had disappeared and was immediately replaced with feelings of love and adoration when Jill finally held Tatum. Grant also remembered that he was the first to cry. When he saw his wife holding his daughter he just lost it. *Some tough guy*, he thought.

He remembered bending down to kiss each of his girls on the forehead before Jill finally spotted his spilling tears. When she did, she lost it too. Then the two of them held each other with one arm and shared guardianship of Tatum with the other.

Like Jill, Grant wished things could have stayed that way and he knew he had to shoulder a significant amount of the blame. If only he could hold Jill in his arms right now and apologize for all of his mistakes. *There are too many to list,* he acknowledged in his thoughts. *I could start by telling her I'm proud of how good she is at her job. I may be too late. But, I have to try.*

~

By breakfast time, Tatum knew she wasn't going to be able to spend another minute doing anything other than trying to get to her family. She could hardly contain herself as she leapt off of her log in the eating area. She speed-walked as she approached Zorica, the beautiful blonde seventeen year-old who had clearly been in charge of the girls for a long time.

"Zorica," Tatum said eagerly as she planted her hands firmly on her hips, "I need to talk to you."

"What about?" asked Zorica.

"I couldn't sleep last night and..." Tatum started before Zorica interrupted her.

"Nobody sleeps their first night. You'll get used to it in no time and it won't be too long after that, that you'll realize you feel right at home here."

"That's just it," Tatum stated emphatically. "This isn't my home. I don't want to get used to it."

"Everyone feels that way at first."

"You're not listening to me," Tatum said, frustrated.

"Wrong. You're not listening to me and that's the source of your confusion. You need to understand that there simply isn't another option here."

"You're the one who's wrong," Tatum lashed out in defiance.

"If you even think about saying…" Zorica started but this time it was Tatum who interrupted.

"We find our families."

"That's not an option," Zorica snapped.

"I disagree."

"Of course you do. You just got here. You don't get it yet. But, don't worry. You will. The rest of us do."

"Get what?"

"Doesn't matter," Zorica stated with a nauseating air of self-importance. "I'm in charge here and I say it's not an option which means it's not. End of story."

"Or," Tatum offered loudly, "maybe it's just the end of you being in charge. Maybe it's time we elect a leader with the guts to do the right thing!"

~

"I nominate Ray!" Kinsey shouted to the entire crowd of boys who had gathered to watch and listen as the debate heated up. Until that moment, it would have been impossible to know which side of the argument any of them fell on. They showed no emotion, just interest.

But, before Trevor could respond, the crowd erupted in shouting and applause – primarily in favor of Kinsey's suggestion of Ray taking over, rather than in response one way or the other to the idea of going to find their families. The response caused Trevor to promptly shrink back with apprehension as Ray glanced around, taken aback.

Kinsey looked at Ray proudly. His beaming pride came from two different sources. First, he was proud of Ray. Kinsey had connected to Ray very quickly and could tell that Ray was a good person and would make a great leader. In the short time he had known Ray, Kinsey had seen that he had the respect of everyone in that camp and he had earned it by showing respect to those same people. There's an old expression that says 'You get what you give' and it certainly applied in this case.

Second, this moment gave Kinsey a sense of quick, immense personal growth. In just a single day, he had managed to do something he never did back home. He had taken some initiative. The kid who, back home, had worked so hard to disappear into the background was now stepping out and being noticed. He was doing it because something finally became too important for him to sit back and do nothing. He was compelled to make it happen and, in order to do that, he had to demand change. But, before he could demand change in anyone else, he had to make a change himself. He had done exactly that and he hoped his reward would be the very thing that had compelled him in the first place, a reunion with his family.

CHAPTER NINETEEN
Preparation

The community had divided into two camps: those who would be staying behind in fear of Raum, and those who would be setting off to find their loved ones with Max and Grant. Those going on the journey numbered just over fifty, well over half the village.

The first part of the journey would simply be getting to the shoreline. It sounded easy enough but, with rumors of the violent wrath of this Raum character that Grant wasn't so sure he believed even existed, they had to be prepared for anything.

They spent the day gathering supplies but had to be fair and leave food and weapons for those staying behind. They didn't want a physical confrontation before the quest even began. Plus, they simply wanted to do right by the people they had grown to care about after spending so much time with them. Some of them had known each other for years and felt a kinship nearly as close as the loved ones they were headed out in search of. Saying goodbye, when the time came, wouldn't be easy.

The trip to their boat typically took two days. If they ran into any trouble and had to expel time and energy fighting and then treating the wounded, it could take longer. They hoped to be at the shoreline in three days or less.

Once there, they would take the boat used for fishing in the summers and set sail for one of the other islands. The big question was, which island to choose. After much debate, the men agreed to attempt to reach the South island first because the women would likely be of more help in the case of danger than the kids could be. Not everyone agreed with this, partly because not everyone had a woman they thought could be waiting for them in this world, but the logic was sound and majority ruled.

~

So far, the girls had done all of their fishing from the shoreline. But, work on a boat had been ongoing for months. The new plan was to finish it as quickly as possible. To no one's surprise, those staying behind put up a fight in letting the others even take the boat. But, since they were outnumbered, they eventually gave up. Refusing to help, however, they went about business as usual while Tatum and the others scrambled to finish the boat's construction without their help.

Naturally, it wasn't as sophisticated as modern fishing boats, but they hoped it would suffice. It was essentially two canoes connected by logs with a giant wooden raft in the middle. The boat's only source of power would be provided by the girls themselves, who would be rowing with oars.

Moirah approached Tatum hesitantly and spoke, "Tatum?"

"Yeah?" Tatum answered, immediately noticing a timid side of Moirah she hadn't seen yet.

"Can I talk to you?"

"Of course. What's up?"

"In private?" Moirah asked, sheepishly.

"Sure," Tatum said as she finished tying a log down, got to her feet, and walked Moirah thirty yards or so down the beach to get away from everyone. "Everything okay?"

"Yeah," Moirah started before sighing, "Well, no. Not really. I'm thinking… Maybe I should stay."

"What?" Tatum asked, shocked. "Why?"

"I don't really know," Moirah admitted.

"Come on. Be honest. What's stopping you? Don't you have someone that might be out there?"

"Maybe."

"Who?"

"My mom," Moirah said sadly. "It's been a really long time. She and my dad got in a fight. He left. They were so angry at each other and I was angry at both of them because I was so sick of all the endless fighting. He was in a car accident and died. I never forgave her for that. I became angry at just her. We hated each other every day for almost two years. Then I woke up here."

"Do you still feel that way about her?"

Moirah shook her head as she began to cry, "But what if she still does?"

Tatum gave her a hug and whispered, "I'd be willing to bet that you're both ready for resolution."

~

Trevor and a few of his faithful cronies looked on with visible animosity as Ray, Kinsey, and the majority of the community gathered their supplies for the expedition that lay ahead. They were taking over half of the hunting and fishing gear, almost half of the cooking supplies, and even some of the blankets.

It was clear to everyone in Ray and Kinsey's group that the level of anger was escalating among Trevor and his followers. The departing group believed they were in the right and that they were not doing anything to deserve the backlash. All they were taking was what they absolutely needed and, seeing as how their numbers made up over half of the original group, they figured they were entitled to it. If anything, they thought they were being generous with how much they were leaving behind. Obviously, those who had chosen to stay didn't see it that way.

Trying to ignore the resentment, Kinsey attempted to focus on what he was looking forward to. He thought of his bedroom, those cinnamon roll ups his sister made for him, and of course, he thought of all three members of his family. He couldn't keep his smile to himself any longer and finally asked Ray, "What do you miss most from back home?"

"Fully functioning showers and toilets sound pretty good about now."

"Agreed," Kinsey quickly responded.

"But, I think I'd have to go with my toothbrush."

"Really?"

"Yeah, because this thing I've got going on in my mouth right now is a lot like I would guess butt must taste like."

"Gross," Kinsey said through laughter.

Suddenly, but to no one's surprise, the metaphorical resentment pot finally boiled over and Trevor approached Kinsey with an air of hostility and four of his allies in tow. "You did this!" Trevor raged. "We were fine before you showed up. You're ruining everything I've worked for!"

Jill turned to face Diane, an intimidating woman who was significantly over-weight – even for her 5'11" frame, and spoke calmly. "First of all, this isn't about you. And, second, I'm not ruining anything. I'm fixing it."

"Fixing it?" Diane screamed, barely remaining in control of her own emotions. "We've made the most of a tough situation. We got here alone and became a unit. You're destroying a community."

"I'm sure you believe that," Jill admitted sincerely. "But, that's not what's happening here."

"Yes, it is," Diane said firmly. "You're not going to do this to me."

"You?"

"Us. You're not going to do this to us."

"You became a community," Jill continued. "I'll give you that. But, as a community, you've hid in fear. You've hid from your real families and that's utterly shameful. I'll tell you what, since you clearly want to keep making this about you, let's go ahead and make it about you. You're not helping these people. You're not improving anything. All you're doing is causing more damage. Your destruction ends now."

Jill turned to the rest of the group and shouted, "Let's finish packing and get some rest! We leave at dawn!"

CHAPTER TWENTY
A World Aware

Like a plant, every person begins as a seed. Each seed contains the genetic make-up, passed on through the generations of family members in the lineage of the father who produced that seed.

It is then placed in the mother's womb where it adds the genetic make-up from her lineage. The mother of all plants is the earth itself and, therefore, that womb is the soil the earth provides. For people, the womb is inside the mother's abdomen.

Both wombs provide protection from the outside environment so that the seed can grow and start the process of becoming what it was created to be. Inside both wombs, the seed is provided with the nourishment required to mature into the plant or person it needs to become before it is ready to enter the outside world.

However, once the plant or person has entered that world, it is not meant to be detached from its mother just yet. The plant still has its roots embedded in the womb it came from and the person, while not physically, still does as well.

Both continue receiving nourishment from their mother. The plant still gets it directly from its mother's womb. The person, however, can then be fed by either parent. Or, even another person.

In the outside world, the protection of the mother's womb has significantly decreased. Both plants and people are still growing into what they were created to be but that growth is determined by additional factors. Not the least of which, physically for the plant and spiritually for the person, is how much exposure they have to both the light and the dark.

~

The darkness was suddenly interrupted by the sun's light peeking over the horizon, setting in motion the dawn of a new day, a new adventure, and a new era.

Tatum, Moirah, and the rest of the girls who planned to take the voyage, stepped out of their huts and immediately headed to the boat so they could get back to work. There was an air of unified determination amongst the group. But, even more important was the feeling of anticipated joy the girls were experiencing. It had been ushered into the group by a critical piece of the human experience that had been absent for a long time: hope.

As they approached the boat, Tatum was surprised by the light touch of a hand between the shoulder blades on her back. "How can I help?" Zorica asked.

Tatum turned around and smiled with pure joy at the unusually faint-hearted expression on Zorica's face. It was the first time Tatum had seen any expression of humbleness from the once dominant force among the girls. She didn't bother to wonder what had changed Zorica's attitude. She simply accepted the change for what it was: A huge leap in the right direction. Accordingly, instead of an answer, Tatum delivered a heart-felt hug.

~

The goodbye that morning had been every bit as difficult as the boys had anticipated it would be. A number of the boys had stayed inside their sleeping quarters. To no one's surprise, Trevor and his cronies were among them. It was anger and bitterness that kept them inside. Others who didn't come out, it was assumed, just didn't want to face their friends and the sadness that seeing them go would bring. Or, they didn't want to face the disappointment they felt in themselves for not having the courage to go with them. For those who did come out, handshakes, high-fives, fist-bumps and hugs were exchanged along with more than a few tears. But, soon, the departure could be delayed no longer.

Kinsey, Ray, and the boys who had joined them, quickly found themselves about a quarter of a mile outside of camp. They were bunched in groups of two or three but, otherwise, were hiking in a fairly consistent line along the established trail.

The sun was almost up and the array of oranges, purples, yellows, blues, and reds that coated the sky made them feel as though this journey was being welcomed by a force greater than they had ever known. While that might have been true, they would soon learn that it was also absolutely unwelcomed by another dreadfully powerful force in Raum.

The saying "ignorance is bliss" was in full evidence and, although they were well aware of the rumors about Raum, the group that had gathered consisted of those who either didn't believe in Raum at all or felt the risk was worth the potential reward. Therefore, they merely shared with one another their admiration for the beautiful sky and their excitement about the possibility of a reunion with those they loved.

~

"I think this is the first time I've noticed how gorgeous it is out here," admired Jill.

"It is," agreed Elaine before turning her attention to a more personal topic of conversation. "So, I haven't even heard who it is you think might be out here."

"My son," Jill contemplated. "Kinsey. He's nine. He's the most likely one. He disappeared and I was looking for him right before I woke up here. My husband and daughter were with me so, I suppose they could be here, too."

"Wow," Elaine said in a more somber tone than the word is typically uttered. "Four of you, huh?"

"Maybe," Jill thought out loud.

"For me it's just my daughter," Elaine offered with a sweet and sour combination of hope and fear. "Her father died quite a while back and, I guess neither of us ever really got over it."

"I don't know if anyone ever does get over something like that, do they?"

"I'm still trying but, probably not."

"Hopefully we'll get to see the ones we still have soon enough though," Jill exclaimed, trying to add a positive spin on the conversation.

"Hopefully."

After a few moments of silence, Jill finally broke it with a new thought, "Too bad Diane and her clique refused to come."

"It is?" Elaine asked, taken aback.

"Of course," Jill admonished kindly. "She needs her loved ones as much as any of us do."

"I guess so," Elaine considered. "Still, I prefer to make this trek with the group we have."

"I won't argue with that. Not for a second."

~

Following along the side of a small river, Grant and his crew had trudged on through the valley and worked their way into a dense forest. The tall, thick growth had crowded out a lot of the sunlight. Though it was darker, the sun was shining brightly and managed to pierce the forest in sporadic rays that caused the men to squint until they passed them. But, the warmth they felt from the sun trumped the sting in their eyes and caused them to want to linger in it as long as they could without coming to a stop.

They lugged their gear along the same path taken every Summer when it was time to go deep sea fishing but, this was the first time they had made the expedition in the Fall. The leaves were changing colors and beginning to litter the ground. It was a beautiful sight and they hoped they had made the journey enough times that they wouldn't lose their way.

They would soon find out that the leaves on the ground were

the least of their worries. Behind the last man in line, the trees and the bushes had begun turning to watch them go while they waited for a command from Raum.

PART FIVE
Pushing Through

CHAPTER TWENTY-ONE
Know Your Enemy

"So, let me make sure I understand this correctly," Jill said to Elaine while staring off into the jungle and eating a handful of stunningly deep purple berries that she had pulled from the bright red branches next to her only seconds earlier.

They were taking a short break from their travels to rest up a bit. It was the first break since they'd left the camp a couple of hours earlier. Some needed to rest their feet while others needed a snack and a few were in need of a bathroom break – not that there were any bathrooms nearby. The privacy of some bushes for cover is all anyone could hope for. Little did they know, in this world, the plants themselves were watching.

"Hit me," Elaine responded as she reached in front of Jill and picked a few berries for herself. She lifted her cupped hand to the middle of her face and inhaled the distinct odor the berries gave off, which was a surprising but delightful combination of peach and honey, while Jill continued to speak.

"We've got this tyrannical god/devil/demon thing everyone calls Raum that rules this place like some kind of monarch/totalitarian/dictator guy."

"A little redundant but, otherwise, you're on the right track so far," Elaine told Jill as she popped the first berry in her mouth and savored the yummy flavor.

"Thanks," Jill blurted sarcastically as she briefly got sidetracked. "What does Raum mean, anyway?"

"No clue."

"It means no clue? Or, you don't know what it means?"

"The latter," Elaine shot back with a smirk. "I don't have the foggiest idea what it means. Never really even given it much thought. For all I know it's Greek for Snickerdoodle. Oh, Snickerdoodles sound good…"

"Fair enough. You're right. Snickerdoodles do sound good. Actually, a cookie of pretty much any kind sounds good. But, back to Raum. So, this thing wants us separated from our loved ones so badly that he brings us to this world where he can keep us captive on different islands even though he has to have us on the brink of disconnection in our own world first."

"Right."

"Divorce or people not talking to each other, those things

aren't enough?"

"Things like divorce or mere silence still allow a chance, no matter how small, for reconciliation. This place doesn't."

"Didn't."

"What?"

"This place didn't. We're about to change that."

"Yes, we are."

~

"Together," Ray began adding, "we're stronger than we are apart. You take the love out of our lives and we grow weaker. These are truths as old as the hills. The thing to tag on to them, in this place, is the fact that the weaker we are, the stronger Raum is."

"So," Kinsey presumed, "the stronger we are, the weaker Raum is."

"I think flipping it around like that makes a lot of sense," Ray agreed. "If one is true, and I know it is, then the other must be, too."

"Then we're weakening Raum right now by banding together."

"Not so fast. Our group just got cut in half because not everyone wanted to go on this quest of yours. I can't say I know if we've made Raum weaker or stronger by doing that. Only time will tell."

"Good point. Either way, this is the part I really don't get."

"What?"

"Everyone was just cool with letting Raum get stronger while we stayed weak?"

"Of course not. I already told you, you're not the first to suggest an adventure like this."

"So, what happened before that made everyone bow down?"

"I don't know about bowing down," Ray argued. "Whipped, maybe. Like a dog. Defeated."

"How? What happened?"

"Other than the obvious?" Ray asked. "People died, man. At some point you just get tired. Then you rest for a while and either give up or you forget how hard the fight was and start fighting all over again – which is exactly what we're doing right now."

"We will get tired again though," Kinsey conceded.

"Yes, we will. But, maybe this time, so will Raum."

"We have to keep pushing until he does."

"So, this time, we will. Different group, different result."

~

"You know, Max" Grant started in, "there are a lot of

expressions out there about the binding nature of yin and yang."

"Can't say I know what you mean, buddy," Max replied.

"They say without sorrow, you can't know joy. You can't gain confidence without first feeling fear. Without understanding the consequences of death, you won't truly respect life. And, you can't know love until you've become familiar with loss."

"I see the common thread but I'm still not sure I know where you're headed with this, Grant."

"Two things. First, if this Raum does exist and is ruling this world, wanting to keep us split up and captive, then there's someone or something else out there wanting us together and free."

"Interesting thought. What's the other thing?"

"If Raum wants us separated from love, feeling alone and fearing his wrath and the consequences that it brings – including death – then the yin to his yang allows him to bring us here so that we can conquer Raum and learn to respect the lives we have, finding joy by returning to the love we were meant to have all along. Like a muscle, we have to be torn down and grow weak so that we can come back even stronger. That being the case, Raum's no longer the most powerful force in this place. Right? And, since love conquers hate and good conquers evil, I'd go so far as to say he's not the most powerful force in Kadosh. Something out there is even more powerful. We find a way to harness that and we beat Raum 6 days a week and twice on Sunday."

"Better safe than sorry. That's another saying I've often heard. I don't know if either Raum or the yang to his yin exists but, just in case, I'm glad we decided to team with your guy."

~

"I wouldn't risk my life," Tatum stated emphatically, "let alone everyone else's lives, if I didn't think success was possible."

"I know you wouldn't," Moirah conceded as they walked along the beautiful sandy beach, each in silent reflection. After a moment, Moirah couldn't help but add, "It's still easier said than done. That's all."

"Always true," Tatum admitted while turning her head to look back out over the gorgeous water. "Always."

Practically in unison, they stopped walking and faced the water, side-by-side, as if they each knew that they were now taking in the last moments of the closest thing to peace that Kadosh could offer. Still looking at the vast ocean in front of them, Tatum reached her left arm up behind Moirah and placed her hand on Moirah's left shoulder while slowly dropping her head to the side and resting it on Moirah's right shoulder. Moirah felt comforted and leaned her head to rest the side of it on the top of Tatum's. Everything was silent accept for one last sentence from Tatum who quietly, and she hoped prophetically, whispered, "It'll be worth it."

They were surrounded by life both on land and in the sea that continued to watch and listen to their every move and word, knowing full-well what neither Tatum nor Moriah possibly could: Raum had already delivered the command for an attack.

CHAPTER TWENTY-TWO
The First Assault

The first assault commanded by Raum would not be instigated by the plants, nor the trees, nor any vegetation at all, for that matter. Their time would come. But, this wasn't it. An assault, however, was imminent. In fact, the time for Raum's first attack on the quest from the four corners of Kadosh had arrived.

Suddenly, all of the women stopped in their tracks. Their bodies were temporarily frozen in fear but their heads started to swivel. There was no mistaking it; they'd all heard the sounds of something approaching. However, they all looked in different directions as though they couldn't tell where the sounds had come from. In order to gain wider lines of vision, the women forced their bodies to loosen up so they could turn in a full circle.

Jill turned to look at the befuddled group, then turned back around. When she first turned away, the path had been empty.

That was no longer the case. Her heart felt like it had dropped into her stomach at the sight of the creature now standing in front of her. Drooling from its mouth and baring its teeth, was a Bengal Tiger bigger than any she had ever seen in any zoo with the possible exception of a huge Siberian Tiger that she once saw on a trip to San Diego with her family.

Had it been in a cage and posing no threat, the animal would have appeared beautiful with its slender legs, orange and brown coloring perfectly accented by the fine white fur on the cheeks, mouth, eyebrows, and abdomen, and the numerous black stripes. Instead, the menacing beast in front of them looked as though it weighed more than 600 pounds, hadn't eaten in days, and viewed them as exactly the feast it had been waiting for.

As the women behind Jill noticed the growling beast, who easily stood above their waist level and had to be 10 feet long, there were gasps followed by frozen silence. For a moment, no one knew what to do. Then, slowly, and without a common call or command, they all began to draw weapons and ready themselves for battle.

~

Kinsey and the other boys stared down the 1,500 pound, dark brown, Kodiak bear with a strange but understandable combination of both apprehension and determination. The bear stared back at them like they were not a group of boys in the forest but a giant school of salmon in a stream, ready to be devoured. Without any warning, the eye contact was cut off and the crippling silence abruptly ended.

Nearly everyone took a step back as the Kodiak roared and stood on its hind legs, towering above the boys at a solid and imposing height of 10 feet. As wide-eyed as they were, the boys planted themselves firmly in the ground and gripped their weapons like safety blankets, as ready for an attack as they could possibly be.

"Ready", however, is a very relative term. Sure, their weapons were drawn and they were facing their enemy. But, "ready" doesn't account for the deep fear that each one of the boys was experiencing. Some had hands that were shaking, others felt sweat beads form on their brows, and at least half a dozen boys suddenly felt the urge to urinate. Luckily, no one wet his pants.

The boys took another step back as the bear dropped to all fours and stopped growling. There was a silent pause, which felt to the boys like it lasted for minutes but was actually only a few seconds long, while they silently wondered what the bear would do next. The bear answered that question their curiosity by thunderously roaring again, causing a group-wide flinch of terror.

Suddenly, the beast began to charge. Without hesitation, arrows soared. Most missed, three nicked the bear, and one deeply penetrated the left shoulder. But, none of the arrows slowed his formidable advance.

~

Max was the first to swing a spear at the 200 pound, silvery-grey colored cougar. He struck it in the rib-cage, sending the nine-foot long body sprawling sideways with all four paws, claws exposed, ripping violently through the air. One of the claws swiped a man's chest, tearing his shirt and severely scratching his skin, which immediately began to bleed profusely.

The cat hit the ground and, with remarkable agility, was back on its feet uttering a low-pitched hissing sound that quickly evolved into a rumbling growl before anyone could put another stick on it.

Taking swipes at the nervous men who surrounded him, the cougar's ears remained erect but he seemed to point at his prey with his powerful neck and jaw while he bared his teeth, promising death to anyone who dared to threaten him.

Max, Grant, and several other men somehow found the courage to confront the cougar with everyone else behind them for back up. But, blow for blow, the cougar would swipe with one paw, the men would jab at him with their spears, and the cougar would bat the spears away with the other paw. The tired but determined men seemed to be getting nowhere. Had there been time to despair, the men surely would have done so. Instead, they continued to fight. Unfortunately, they were losing the battle which could possibly cost them their lives.

~

Even with the danger that confronted her, Tatum couldn't help but remember the way that her mother had shielded her and shooed away a vicious dog who had frightened her when she was a sobbing five year-old girl. The comfort of that protective parental guardianship role, which seems to come naturally to most parents when their children are threatened, was completely absent in this world and was sorely missed.

Tatum, of course, wished her mother was here to help her now as she watched the 50-foot long, 1,000 pound Reticulated Python swallow a girl whole. Screaming from the onlookers was all that could be heard. Those who weren't hysterical were throwing rocks or beating the giant reptile with sticks.

One girl ventured close enough to stab the Python, and it retaliated by wrapping her up and squeezing her so hard that she couldn't breathe. As the girl turned a pale shade of blue, the other girls scrambled to free her, but the snake was too strong. They continued their attack but their efforts seemed hopeless until Zorica threw a spear that penetrated the snake under its mouth only an inch or two above the bulge created by the ingested adolescent, went up through its head and came out on the other side.

The severity of the wound caused the snake to writhe in pain and to release the suffocating girl. The giant body then collapsed to the ground where it lay lifeless.

All eyes shifted to Zorica who quipped, "How does snake sound for dinner?"

CHAPTER TWENTY-THREE
An Uncommon Adversary

With the trees and plants still watching, Kinsey and Ray sat next to one another while the entire camp feasted on the Kodiak meat they had roasted over the fire. Most of the conversation was centered on their victory over the bear they were now eating. They had already relived Will's triumphant spear through the side moment about a dozen times. That spear, they assumed, had punctured the bear's heart and abruptly ended the threat. Now they were feasting on their conquest.

Kinsey had noticed a lack of food smell as it cooked. He expected to smell a distinct odor of some sort but it simply smelled like a campfire. The campfire aroma was very pleasant, but surprising nevertheless.

His attention had since moved on to the flavor on his tongue, which had also surprised him. "So much for everything tasting like chicken," he said to the group, who responded with a collective chuckle. Kinsey took another bite. "This is unique."

"Good though," responded Will, another boy sitting near-by who seemed more at home in this environment than most of the others. "Like venison, only better."

"Venison?" Kinsey asked.

"Deer."

"Oh," Kinsey pondered before asking a follow up question. "Have you eaten a lot of deer?"

"Some. More back home than here though."

"Where's home?" Kinsey inquired.

"Penuel, Wyoming. It's a small town in Sweetwater County. Not too far from Granger. We do a lot of huntin' out there."

"Got it. Makes sense. I'll be honest, though. Other than Wyoming, none of the places you just mentioned sound even a little bit familiar. How long have you been here?"

"Maybe seventy years or so," Will answered with a bit of sadness.

"Seventy years?" Kinsey responded, taken aback. It was the longest period of time he'd heard of so far.

"That's why I had to go with you this time," Will acknowledged, still expressing his sorrow.

"What do you mean, this time?"

"I stayed behind the last time a group decided to try and find their families," Will admitted. "I've regretted it ever since. I promised myself I wouldn't make that mistake twice."

"Looking forward to tomorrow then?" asked Ray.

"I've waited way too long for this. I'm looking forward to the whole trip. Come what may."

~

Once again, Jill and the other women were awakened by the morning sunlight. This morning, however, the sun wasn't quite as brilliant as it had been the previous day. Faint grey clouds had crowded the sky and the sun seemed to actually be fighting to break through as if the clouds had taken a defensive stance and fortified a rampart that was nearly impossible to penetrate. The sky was darker, but not yet threatening a storm, just shielding the sunlight and its inviting warmth.

Typically, the lack of alluring sunlight would make the waking up process slow and lethargic. However, these determined women needed no additional motivation. Waking up was like a contagious chain-reaction. The stirring of one led to the stirring of a few, and the stirring of a few led to the stirring of all. In a matter of just a few short minutes, soon after the completion of the days new dawn, they were all on their feet.

As they re-packed their things, the women continued talking

about the fear the tiger had instilled in them the day before. They were thankful for the rock Jill had thrown that hit the tiger between the eyes and stunned it long enough for a woman named Amy to bravely slit its throat. But, their conversation was primarily still about how scary the whole situation was.

As they packed and talked, they nibbled on a variety of fruits that included zebra bananas, sugar apples, and baby papayas. They ate on the go because they were anxious to continue their journey. They were fed, hydrated, and successfully back on the trail in less than an hour from the first stirring.

The women marched toward their boat with purpose. In addition to thoughts about the terrifying tiger, each of their minds drifted back to exclusive memories with a common theme: the love of their respective families. These memories were the fuel that kept their bodies in motion and the further down the trail they got, the more they visualized creating new memories with those same family members.

~

Moirah nearly shivered with the onset of a sudden eerie feeling that she and the other girls were being watched. She slowly set the supplies down on the boat and peered past the trees beyond the beach, half expecting to spot a party of wild savages on the hunt. Instead, all she saw were the trees, bushes, and tall grass that were always there. Still, she couldn't shake the unnerving feeling that someone or something was stalking them.

"You okay?" Tatum asked, noticing Moirah's inquisitive stare at the same time as a light, cool breeze swirled around them that caused each of them to experience a short but, very real and vibrant shiver.

"What? Oh, yeah. I'm fine. I just have a really weird feeling."

"What kind of really weird feeling?"

"I'm not sure," Moirah responded hesitantly. "It kind of feels like someone's watching us work."

"You mean the girls who aren't coming with us?"

"No. Someone else. Someone we're not even aware of."

Tatum suddenly began to feel the same weird sensation, as if she had quickly caught a rapidly spreading virus. "Well, that's spooky."

"Very spooky."

Tatum looked out at the tree line Moirah was staring into. She scanned the same bushes and tall grass Moirah had been staring at but didn't see anything out of the ordinary. She brought her attention back to where she stood and briefly studied Moirah. A clear sensation of anxiety had washed over her. "Have you had that feeling before?"

"Not like this."

"Everyone's felt like they were being watched before though, right?"

"This is different."

"Awesome," Tatum stated with a heavy dose of sarcasm.

"Yeah," Moirah agreed as she gazed back through the trees. "Awesome."

~

The two spears that had struck the attacking cougar weren't thrown. They were both still in hand as Max stuck the cat in the rib cage from one side and a man named Isaac stuck it in the stomach from the other. But, the conversation about their eventful battle with the cougar had essentially ended long before the men had re-entered the trail.

Having walked for about ninety minutes that morning, Grant suddenly stopped, causing the other men to stop, too. He stared pensively at a tree off to the side of the path.

"What is it?" Max asked.

"I swear that tree just moved," Grant answered.

"There's a little breeze going right now. Trees do that," Max said with a bit of a grin.

"Not what I mean," Grant responded with a smile that was just enough to be friendly but also told Max that Grant was serious and that this was something worth paying attention to.

"Okay. What do you mean?" asked Max.

"It didn't sway. It turned."

"Turned? Like swiveled?"

"Exactly."

"Okay. Trees don't to that. That's just not possible."

"Being here's not possible."

"Good point," Max admitted with a sigh as he transitioned from skepticism to a deep concern. "Are you sure you saw what you think you saw?"

"Pretty sure."

"What do you want to do about it?"

"Nothing we can do. Let's just keep moving. Eyes and ears open."

"Agreed. Let's do it," Max affirmed.

They started walking again and, as the last of the men walked out of view of the tree in question, it twisted toward them, then away, checking to see if the coast was clear, and then turned back around as if signaling another soldier.

Slowly and quietly, a large boulder rolled out from behind the tree and onto the path that the men were walking on. It continued to roll until it reached the other side of the path and connected with another, even bigger, boulder. Once that connection was secure, the first boulder slid up the path while the second remained stationary. Then, the first boulder remained stationary while the second boulder slid around it. This repeated several times as the boulders worked together to walk themselves up the path until they connected with a third boulder, then a fourth, and so on. Something was clearly assembling behind the men. It was big. It was menacing. And, it had been sent by Raum.

CHAPTER TWENTY-FOUR
An Uncommon Adversary

The 120 foot tall emergent tree tucked its canopy of small pointed leaves into its slimy, moss-covered trunk like a closing umbrella. It quietly but swiftly shrunk to a tenth of its original height. As it did, it grew wider while shedding pieces of its brown and gloomy bark covering like a prisoner finally breaking free of its chains after a long, harsh sentence. In one fell swoop, it reached its modified size and leaned forward, with its branches becoming like centipede legs and the leaves became like porcupine quills, as it stealthily hit the ground.

With moss dangling from its legs, the sinister creature quietly scurried up the trail toward the pack of women. The faintest pitter-patter of the creature's emaciated feet on the ground was audible but so muffled, that it couldn't be heard by human ears. The long, dense body had been a stiff tree trunk only seconds ago but now had the agility of a serpent as if hundreds of dormant vertebrae and ribs had suddenly been activated. The movement came in rapid waves that started in the back and sprang up and forward until disappearing as it reached the side-winding head and then started all over again.

The creature's head was covered in hanging moss resembling the greasy hair of a sweaty rock star at the end of a three-hour concert, which made the solid white eyes in the front stand out like a pair of flashlights in a dark tunnel.

Slinking in behind the women unnoticed, the huge and menacing creepy-crawler had every intention of pleasing its master, the infamous Raum, by catching the women by surprise and making sure their journey came to an abrupt and fatal end.

~

The ferocious monster stalking Tatum and the other girls was something akin to a lion but clearly derived from a palm tree - distinguished by its large, compound, feather-leaved, evergreen foliage stemming from the top and reaching back down its narrow but muscular body like an extra-long mane.

When it finally decided to make its presence known, the monster's leaves rustled noisily as they fanned out like a peacock's feathers and its mouth made a popping sound similar to the unsticking of a suction cup as it unsealed and opened wide, showing hundreds of long, pointed teeth that made a complete circle in the middle of its head. The brash noise that followed was half roar and half screech, causing the girls to look back and freeze in silent panic.

They looked on as the racket calmed and the monster's mouth closed. It deliberately lowered its head, as if preparing to charge, like a bull staring down the matador and his red cape. But, before it could be ready to launch itself, the monster blinked its brown eyes and wooden horns suddenly raised out of the top of its skull. They were close to two feet in length, smooth and solid like brown elephant tusks, and came to an extremely sharp point at the tip. The girls looked on in wonderment. No one had ever seen horns grow before their eyes. Of course, none of them had ever seen anything like this at all. With only a split second to think, it became abundantly clear to the girls that the receiving end of a blow from those horns was a bad place to be. The temporary sense of wonderment was gone as quickly as it had come and fear was immediately back at the front of the emotional line.

The leaves began to rustle again as the monster next began to slowly display a pair of mass clusters of hundreds of small, black, star-shaped flowers that quickly developed into very impressive wings.

The monster, now fully prepared to do battle, stared his prey down in a successful attempt to intimidate the now completely freaked-out group of girls.

~

Grant, Max and the other men stared in terror at the foreboding, colossal, ogre-like giant with a human form; but instead of bones, muscles and skin, it was made entirely of course rocks. It deliberately rotated its head from side-to-side as if it was checking out the individual members of the group, but no eyes were visible on the giant. In fact, it had no mouth, no nose, and no ears either. At least, not as far as the men could tell.

As if just to prove it meant business, the giant grabbed a huge rock with each hand and then smashed them together in front of him and shattered them into thousands of smaller pieces.

"That's a little self-loathing," Max quipped.

"A little bit," Grant responded while still focused on the giant in front of them. "Think he'll just commit suicide?"

"At the moment, I don't feel that lucky. You?"

When it followed the display by reaching one leg out in front of the other in what turned out to be a ground-shaking step forward, the men all took a corresponding reactive step backward.

"Not really," Grant answered without having ever taken his eyes off of the giant.

Unfortunately, in addition to making less of an impact on the ground beneath them, the men's steps were significantly smaller than the giant's. So, as the process continued, it became increasingly evident that the men were going to have to either turn and run or stay and do battle.

As the two options became evident, they all realized that no one had any clue as to how to fight this powerful giant. Therefore, any kind of a battle was beginning to look like a very bad idea.

~

Kinsey and the other boys scattered as the beast charged over the ground where they had just been. Frozen in fear, they looked on and stared blankly putting their trepidation on full display.

The beast itself had clearly evolved from the terrain. It had taken the form of some kind of an odd stegosaurus and wild boar hybrid. It was easily twelve feet in length from the tip of its snout to the base of its tail. However, its body looked as though it had been made out of rich dirt and covered in blades of green grass. Its tail was like a small bouquet of dried out silky lupine. As if that didn't make the beast look crazy enough, inexplicably large, flat, kite-shaped dermal plates, that looked as though they'd been hastily carved out of diorite rocks, armored the beast from the head to the tail, like shingles scattered all over its rounded back.

Even its vicious-looking teeth, with muddy slobber dripping off the rough edges, seemed to be recklessly chiseled from stone – including the tusk-like canine teeth that stood out from the bottom front of its mouth like upside down fangs thirsty for blood. But, the scariest feature was its eyes. They were an angry, violent shade of red and looked like fire could shoot out of them at any moment.

Someone better come up with a plan quick, Kinsey thought as the dreadful beast charged at the group, enraged and fully equipped to run through the group and knock everyone around like bowling pins. *If we don't, we're all dead.*

CHAPTER TWENTY-FIVE
Another Round of Killing

Most of the men were now fearfully running away from the charging rock-monster. A few had started climbing up the face of a mountain. Grant, the one leading that small group, had just reached a ledge a few yards above what would be the monster's eye level if the monster had been sporting any eyes. The most important feature of the ledge Grant was pulling himself onto was the large boulder that rested on it.

A patch of grass with a single flower, a buttercup, looked out of place hidden behind the boulder - especially since there was no water in sight. But, its untouched appearance suggested that it had been protected by the giant rock for quite some time. Grant did not have time to concern himself with the buttercup. This well rested boulder was about to be awakened because it was the only weapon they had with any chance of success in the battle they now found themselves in.

Grant helped Max and the others up onto the ledge, noticing the huge ravine on the opposite side of the trail below them. *That could be helpful,* he thought to himself.

"What are we doing?" Max asked Grant.

"Helping this thing commit suicide," Grant answered just before quickly shouting down to the others retreating, "Circle back around!"

Though some of them thought he had absolutely lost his mind, they hadn't come this far to retreat if they thought there was any chance of success. So, they heard the order, assumed Grant had a plan, hoped for the best and did what they'd been told to do. Changing course caused the rock-monster to stop his forward momentum and begin to turn, squaring its massive body more in line with the men on the hill.

"Get in here and give it all you've got," Grant instructed as he put his back against the face of the mountain. He raised his feet up over the flower that was about to lose its shield and placed his feet on the boulder. "We're only going to get one shot at this!"

~

As the snarling beast turned around and began to return for another charge, the boys got back up on their feet and launched everything they had at it. Spears, arrows, and even rocks flew through the air. The rocks bounced off of it, but they hoped that the impact was felt anyway, and some of the arrows and spears ricocheted off of the dermal plates. However, several arrows and a couple of spears penetrated the grassy layer and stuck in the earthy body.

Each incursion caused a smoke-like dust cloud, rather than drawing blood. But, in spite of not seeing any blood, the boys had to believe that they were making progress in slowing the beast down. Eventually, the wounds would have to prove fatal and bring the beast to a stop. They had to hold on to the hope that they could keep up the effort and, ultimately, outlast their assailant.

~

Tatum stared at the lion-like creature as it's mane of leaves folded back down its body, creating an aero-dynamic suit while its face sprang forward in severe pain. The creature's mouth opened wide again, showing its full circle of ferocious teeth, as the half roar and half screech sound once again discharged angrily out of its ghastly mouth.

Face still stretched forward and body wounded but ready to attack again, the creature slowly closed its mouth and grew eerily quiet as it carefully scanned the girls and began to raise its wings.

~

The women watched like a battalion of soldiers waiting to see if their enemy would attack again or surrender. The decision to use the break to reload their weaponry turned out to be a smart one because the answer was not the one they would have hoped for.

The menacing, white-eyed creature with a body covered in moss drooping from dark, gothic-looking bark and centipede-like legs underneath made from branches suddenly began to charge one more time.

~

The flying creature was now airborne and headed directly at the girls. Its massive mouth was wide open and all of its teeth were showing. That same horrible screeching roar pierced the air at a volume that drowned out the sound of the flapping wings made of inflorescences covered in hundreds of small, black, star-shaped flowers. The girls would have covered their ears if they hadn't been so determined to kill the violent creature. So, instead of shielding themselves from the noise, they once again took aim at its source.

~

Rocks, arrows and spears immediately began to fly once more and with similar results. The rocks likely caused a bit of pain but they bounced off with little effect. The arrows and spears often missed but a couple more penetrated the grassy layer of the beast's body and pierced it.

The boy named Will was bitten in the arm and the beast latched on like a vicious, snarling dog. Its eyes somehow seemed to grow even redder as its clinching teeth dug deeper. If Kinsey had, had time to focus on it, he might have wondered if the blood the beast drew from the boy was causing it.

Instead, Kinsey and another boy grabbed the beast by the snout and tried to pry it off while Ray and several others continued stabbing it, hoping it would release its grip and collapse to the ground. Unfortunately, while the air filled with clouds of dust, it felt like the release would never happen.

~

The tumbling boulder had picked up a tremendous amount of speed and, as the giant finished his 180 degree turn in an attempt to keep up with the men circling back to where they had first seen him, it finally reached level ground and struck the rock-monster directly in the right leg. The boulder soared right through the giant and off of the cliff behind it, sweeping both of its legs out from under it on the way through. The giant hit the ground so hard it would have registered on the Richter scale, landing with most of its body hanging over the cliff. The weight was too much for the rock monster and it slid off of the cliff, following the boulder hundreds of feet before shattering on the ground below the same way the rocks in the giant's hands had done just minutes earlier.

~

While most beasts would have fallen to the ground and bled, the earthy boar hit the ground and lost its beastly shape. What was left when the huge dust cloud dissipated into the air, looked like someone had simply dumped out a container of yard waste and laid a spear on top of it. The pile was mostly dried out leaves and grass blades with a small pile of mud where the beast's head had been.

The boys looked at each other, confused. Finally, Ray exclaimed, "Only in Kadosh, right?"

~

Jill and several other women stood over the tree on the ground that looked like it had been dead for years. It was broken into several pieces from the women had chopped through the trunk like they were making firewood. "This one would make a lousy dinner," she told the group. "Let's gather ourselves, treat the wounded and move on. Be aware out here. There's no telling what Raum will send next."

CHAPTER TWENTY-SIX
Resolve

Kinsey helped a couple of the boys to their feet. Several of them had been knocked down by the earthy beast and would likely suffer a few bruises but Will was the only one with a serious injury. The bite had been painful and scary. The fear of having his arm in the beast's lockjaw-like grip was gone now but that allowed Will to focus on the pain, making it feel substantially worse than it had when the beast had the vulnerable arm in its snarling clutch.

"You okay?" Ray asked Will, looking down at Will's bleeding limb.

"I will be," Will responded bravely but with a bit of a grimace. "I just need to find some jewelweed. Crush it up and cover my arm in it."

That was good news to Ray because it meant the injury would

not affect the rest of their journey in the physical sense. However, between the attack of the Kodiak bear and now the second attack by this bizarre half boar, half dinosaur beast, a lingering fear was clearly eroding the over-all confidence level of the group.

"Jewelweed?" Kinsey inquired, confused. "Isn't that for, like, poison ivy?"

"Yeah," Will explained. "It won't really heal it but it's going to keep it from flaming up and, hopefully, it'll block any toxins that could sneak in while it does heal."

"Good to know," Kinsey acknowledged.

Suddenly, a boy named Andy shouted, "This is your fault!"

Kinsey spun around and saw the boy marching toward him, pointing his finger. Instantly, Kinsey felt both afraid and embarrassed. The spotlight was on him and he wasn't exactly receiving an award.

"You started this whole thing," the boy continued. "You're going to get us all killed!"

Kinsey felt like his heart had sunk to his toes. He was speechless.

Luckily, Ray stepped into Andy's path and stopped him from approaching Kinsey. "Nobody forced anyone to do anything," Ray interjected both to settle the group and protect his new friend. "You decided to do this. We all did. Ask yourself why. We all need to take a minute and remember why we started this journey in the first place so we don't forget how important it is to continue on. Now, let me hear you say it. Why did you start this journey?"

~

"My family," answered a girl named Naomi as the girls' thoughts shifted gears. It had been a roller coaster of emotions over the last few minutes. The fear the creature had created in their hearts was replaced with victorious jubilation when Moirah knocked it out of the sky and the girls were able to overwhelm it. But, then fear had quickly crept back in as thoughts of what other things Raum could send their way set in. It was now time to overcome fear once again.

"Exactly," agreed Moirah with gloominess beginning to dilute as it mixed with fortitude. "I want to find my mom." Moirah scanned the group. "Who else?"

"My dad," answered a girl named Whitney who mustered the courage to explain herself with a heart-felt confession. "The last thing I said to him was that I hated him. I don't. I love my dad. I need to tell him that I didn't mean it. He needs to know that I've missed him like crazy while I've been gone." Tears began to overwhelm Whitney as she said the last of what she could get out. "I love him so much. I just want to go home."

"We all do," agreed Tatum.

The tears were contagious and, collectively, the girls began to well up. Individually, their thoughts drifted to their own families, their own regrets, and the possibility of redemption. The appeal of continuing on was beginning to swell. A shared desire to reunite with loved ones was returning with a rapidly increasing momentum.

Tatum was the newest member of the group but no one felt the desire to go home any more than she did. As the other girls poured their hearts out about their own families, the longing she had for her family amplified all the more. She especially missed her precious, insecure brother and worried how the shy boy would be able to cope in a fear-provoking world like the one she found herself in. It was the very same world she assumed he was in, too. Her concern wasn't just for Kinsey, however, she had to assume they were all trapped in Kadosh and she wondered if this world was too much for any of them – even her stalwart dad.

~

Grant authoritatively addressed the other men, "So, we agree that the risk is worth the reward, right?" Nods and words of affirmation confirmed that the sentiment was unanimous. "Then no more delay. Let's get going," Grant commanded without an ounce of hesitation.

"Let's finish this," Max concurred. The men were once again united in their determination to finish the journey and reunite their families. Emotionally, there are very few forces stronger than the spirit of unification in like-minded people in a noble cause. It was a weapon against the force of Raum, and he was very much aware of it.

"How much further?" Grant probed Max as the men fervently prepared to hit the trail again in spite of the fate that they anticipated awaited at least some, but hopefully not all of them.

"We'll be there in about an hour," Max answered with a hint of uncertainty. He thought for a moment, suffering from an inner debate about the consequences of speaking out loud what he already knew they were both thinking, then caved in and added, "Barring any more set-backs, of course."

"Of course," Grant reluctantly agreed. He couldn't deny that, in all likelihood, this Raum entity was real and would not be surrendering the fight any time soon. Therefore, the worst of what they would face, was likely still ahead of them.

~

Jill, Elaine, and the other women were back on the trail,

determined as ever.

Jill's mind flooded with thoughts of her family and the fates that they might be suffering. She waded through a barrage of memories before settling in on a tragic one.

Grant and Jill had, had a third child. Quinn was conceived when Tatum was just a year old. Like Tatum, Quinn wasn't planned but he was welcome. They were so excited about the idea of adding a little boy to the bunch. Grant couldn't wait to teach him how to shoot a basketball.

Everything with the pregnancy seemed normal but, when Jill went in for a routine check-up at 8 months, she was informed that the amniotic fluid levels in the sac surrounding the fetus had unexpectedly dipped too low and that the baby had already died.

To make matters worse, the baby was almost fully developed and would have to be delivered. So, the doctors induced labor and Jill had to go through the process of giving birth to her dead child. It was the worst day of her life and, Grant was not only there but he was exactly the man she needed him to be. She knew that if he were here with her now, he would provide much needed strength and comfort once again. Unfortunately, she had no idea where he was. She wasn't even sure he was in this strange world.

As she looked up in the sky, wondering, she realized that massive storm clouds were approaching at an impossibly rapid speed. Suddenly, lightning cracked the sky, followed by thunder so intense that it seemed to shake the entire atmosphere. A droplet of water torpedoed downward from the sky and hit Jill directly in the forehead. Instantly, like a punch to her gut, Jill knew that a whole new kind of chaos was breaking loose.

CHAPTER TWENTY-SEVEN
Hiding

The wind had gone from barely noticeable to easily approaching 100 miles per hour in a matter of minutes. The girls scrambled for shelter. They knew they couldn't hide in their bamboo fashioned homes because two of the flimsy huts had already been ripped to shreds by the high winds right before the terrified girls' eyes.

Tatum, Moirah and Naomi ran frantically into the jungle, fighting not only the winds but the damage they were causing as well. Falling branches whipped by like bullets in an Old West shoot-out and the winds were so strong the girls couldn't keep their eyes open, which meant they were very nearly running blind.

Suddenly, a branch hit Naomi so hard on the left side of her body that she fell over, landing hard on her right side. Immediately, a tall and heavy up-rooted tree settled on the upper portion of her legs and trapped her.

Naomi instinctively let out a loud "Oof!" The pain was immense but she didn't have time to focus on it. "Help!" she yelled with as much volume as she could muster, trying to make sure she could be heard over the raucous sounds of the powerful wind.

The cry for help was loud enough to cause both Tatum and Moirah to stop and look back.

"Naomi!" Tatum yelled in response to the alarm bells that instantaneously began sounding in her head.

They rushed to her aid as quickly as they could and immediately tried to lift the tree off of her legs. It took all of two seconds to realize that it was way too heavy.

"Push!" Moirah yelled.

"I'm trying!" Tatum shouted back.

They stopped briefly to catch their breath. Moirah exhaled a final time as the girls firmed their grip on the course bark. "Again!"

They tried several times but it was useless. "I'm sorry," Moirah told Naomi.

"We can't leave her," insisted Tatum.

"Then what do we do?"

"Just go!" shouted Naomi, over the howling winds. "Go!"

"No!" Tatum maintained.

Moirah gestured to Tatum that there was nothing else they could do. Tatum responded with a look of determination but Moirah was right, there was nothing the two of them could do.

Suddenly, bursting through the forest was the help they needed. Zorica, Whitney, and a girl named Sam immediately spotted their friends at the same exact time that their friends spotted them and were enthusiastically ready to put them to work.

"Nice timing," said Tatum with sincere gratitude.

"Help us push!" Moirah exclaimed.

All five of them grabbed the tree and lifted with every bit of strength they could gather. After what seemed like minutes, the tree slowly started to move and the speed picked up quickly. Finally, the girls pushed it off of Naomi and it hit the ground next to her with a low *thud* that could barely be heard over the roaring wind. Tatum helped Naomi to her feet as quickly as she could.

"Now what?" asked Sam who wore the fear she was feeling on her face like an unfriendly Halloween mask.

"Over there," Zorica commanded, pointing to a sizeable cave as the winds grew even stronger and more terrifying. At that point, any kind of shelter would have looked inviting and the girls took off running, as best as they could in the wind storm, toward the cave without any hesitation.

Thunder and lightning boomed and flashed at rapid speed like an outdoor dance party. The rain fell so hard it stung the women's skin as they hurried into the cave where they hoped they'd find protection from the weather. It was unlike anything any of them had ever experienced.

Jill had always loved the clean smell of fresh rain but this rain was different. The smell was somehow musty and the feeling wasn't one of cleansing but one of nefarious rage. It was a foul, manic, vengeful rain.

As she hunkered down Jill looked behind her, out of the cave's entrance, just in time to see a woman named Helena get struck by lightning. Other than a minor trembling, Helena seemed to suddenly freeze as the electric current struck her body and flowed throughout. When it finally stopped, so did the trembling. The women all gasped as they watched Helena drop limply to the ground, dead.

As Elaine rushed out and checked for a pulse she would soon learn wasn't there, Jill thought about the fact that she had only exchanged a sentence or two of conversation with Helena. It made her feel worse that she hadn't gotten to know her, although she wasn't quite sure why. Maybe she felt that she wouldn't be able to remember the deceased woman properly. Maybe she felt responsible because this journey had been her idea and now it had gotten a woman killed. Or, maybe, guilt was just an emotional response that she had recently grown accustomed to.

~

Grant, Max and the other men huddled together inside the cave as the blizzard concealed everything outside in a deep powdery snow.

"Can't see anything out there," Grant blurted out, staring at what essentially looked like a thick white wall. "Where did this thing come from?"

"Raum," Max answered without missing a beat. "He sent the cougar, that crazy rock thingy, and now this. He'll do whatever it takes to stop us. And, until he does, this stuff will keep coming and every event will be worse than the one before it. If we survive this, I'll hate to see what he does next."

"You're a ray of sunshine, aren't you?" Grant blurted out, sarcastically, both in an attempt to keep the conversation from going too dark and in order to purposely ignore the easier path of giving in to fear and panic.

"I'm just tellin' it like it is," Max responded matter-of-factly without looking at Grant.

"Fair enough. How far away from the boat are we?"

"Not far at all," Max told him. "Maybe a quarter of a mile."

"Well, we've come this far…"

"What's another quarter mile?"

"Exactly. Can't let Raum stop us now, can we?"

"At the very least, we can't go down without a fight."

"Good enough."

~

The earth seemed like it had been quaking violently for minutes and this was the third time it had happened in less than half of an hour. With each quake, the force increased significantly and the duration was drastically extended. This time, the quake would not just end quietly. It would climax vociferously.

All of a sudden, what the boys thought was just a mountain behind them, blew its top. The volcano opened up with a booming noise that seemed to end the earth's tremor with an exclamation point as it allowed hot magma, volcanic ash and a variety of gases to escape from below the surface and out into the atmosphere.

The boys turned toward it and looked on with silent amazement. The emotions were a roller coaster that dipped down to dread and soared skyward into wonderment. Finally, Ray was the first to speak, causing the rollercoaster to come to a screeching halt in a valley of dread.

"I think Raum's officially upset."

CHAPTER TWENTY-EIGHT
No Safe Place

Resting his head against the cold cave wall, Grant's mind drifted back to a Saturday a few years earlier when he had taken Kinsey to work with him. A teenaged boy had come in to apply for a job and he was dressed in all black, reminding Grant of a vampire. Grant's instinct was to give the kid a polite interview and then throw the application in the trash without ever calling him. It was Kinsey who reminded Grant of the old adage not to judge a book by its cover. Grant took his son's advice and the kid turned out to be one of the best employees he'd ever had. In fact, he not only still worked for Grant, he was now the top manager at one of his stores. *Kinsey's a smart kid,* Grant thought with two parts pride and one part regret, *whether he knows it or not. There are a lot of good things about Kinsey that I should have taken the time to make sure he believed about himself. If I get another chance, I won't miss that opportunity ever again.*

While Grant was hoping that his son was alive and well, safe from the wrath of Raum that he was experiencing, the men in the back of the group were the first to hear the growling sound. Grant's mind snapped back to his present situation as he and Max turned to listen to what a dozen or so others had already heard.

At first, all they could see was darkness. Then a pair of light brown eyes began to glow. This caused immediate fear among the men, a fear that increased when a familiar low-pitched hissing sound also emanated from the darkness.

"Not another one," Grant quietly exclaimed.

"Another what?" asked Max. "What is that?"

The question answered itself when the hissing sound once again evolved into a rumbling growl.

"Oh," Max sighed.

The cougar stepped threateningly out of the darkness and in to full view. He had made his presence known with the hissing and growling sounds. Now he was putting on a show so that the visual would make the fear of his presence felt deeply and it was working exactly according to Raum's cunning plan.

~

"Snap!" exclaimed Ray.

The group's attention turned from the volcano to the half dozen Kodiak bears approaching in a crescent-shaped battle line.

"Bears don't travel in packs," Ray complained.

"Sure they do," Andy corrected. "But, the packs are called sloths and it pretty much only happens when there's a bunch of food around."

"Well," Ray retorted, "thanks for the education, Andy. What am I supposed to do with that information? Hand 'em a fork?"

"Bears don't use forks," said Andy, clearly not getting the joke.

"Stay still!" shouted Kinsey, trying to focus the group.

Almost in perfect unison, the bears stood up on their hind legs and roared ferociously.

"Now what?" yelled Andy.

"You're the expert," Ray quipped. "You tell us."

As the bears dropped back down to all fours and began to charge, Kinsey yelled back, "Now we run!"

~

The girls sprinted from the cave back out into the storm with at least a dozen pythons pursuing them that were every bit as big as the one they had already killed.

"Head for the boat!" Zorica shouted.

"You want to get on a boat in the middle of a hurricane?" Sam questioned.

"If we don't," Zorica answered, "Raum wins!"

"Plus," Tatum added with a gesture back to the pythons, "I don't really want to stay here with them. Do you?"

"Ugh!" Sam exclaimed before finally agreeing. "Fine, but these are the worst options ever."

"No one's arguing with you about that," Tatum acquiesced.

"What about the other girls?" Moirah asked.

"They're not after the other girls," Tatum observed. "We'll actually be leading the snakes away from them."

"I'm not sure how to feel about that," Moirah admitted. "Is that supposed to make me feel better, or worse?"

"We get on the boat and everyone has a chance or we stay here and everybody most likely dies."

"Okay. I like your idea better."

The girls had to move slowly, holding on to trees as they fought the high winds. Luckily, the pythons had stopped at the mouth of the cave, afraid of the storm, and were retreating back into the darkness. Raum had simply used them to force the girls back out to where he really wanted them. Now he had them out in the weather with no protection.

~

The women bravely trudged on toward the shoreline through pounding rain accompanied by heavy lightning bolts that threatened electrocution with every strike and nearly deafening thunder.

With almost no visibility, the women hadn't noticed several of the trees around them tucking their leaf canopies into their covered trunks, shrinking to a tenth of their original size, leaning forward onto their branch-made centipede legs and creeping toward them in an all-too familiar fashion.

It wasn't until the monsters came crashing in on all sides that the women realized they were being pursued once again. One woman became so scared she tried to climb a tree but it morphed into one of the monsters and dropped her right back on the ground before shooting its quills at her. Her actions rapidly slowed until she could no longer move and she was left completely helpless.

~

Kinsey and the other boys were fighting all elements on their way to the boat. The earth was trembling again, the volcano was spewing behind them and, they were being chased by both the

Kodiak bears and the boar-like earthy beasts that had joined them like a two-pronged army on the hunt for their enemy.

One boy had already been caught by a bear and killed but the others were able to either fight the pursuers off or out-run them.

Finally, the boat was in sight. There was a brief sense of relief, as though the boat represented safety. However, they quickly noticed that the ocean's swells had become enormous because of the earthquakes and, rather than finally reaching safety, they were about to exchange one dangerous scenario for another. This one actually looked like it could possibly be even worse than the former.

Behind them, they faced hungry bears and a sky that was beginning to shower them with ash. In front of them, they faced a sea that was approaching tsunami status in a boat that was meant for fishing in relatively calm waters. Things were scary in the back and utterly terrifying, bordering on suicidal, in the front. But, they all knew in their hearts that they had to keep going forward. They had already come so far and, if they managed to survive this nearly incomprehensible journey, their families could possibly be their reward for risking, and already in some cases, losing their lives.

Without another word spoken, just one foot in front of the other, the steps they were all physically taking demonstrated that, unanimously, they all believed it was worth the risk. So, they trudged on, facing a challenge beyond anything any of them could ever have imagined possible. And, little did they know, their situation was going to get even worse.

PART SIX
Shared Struggle

CHAPTER TWENTY-NINE
Revelation

The boat looked like a semi-modern rendering of a mid-nineteenth century deep-sea fishing vessel. With the exception of the sails and the rope used to raise and lower them, it was made entirely out of wood. The boat may not have been fancy but it got the job done.

As the women approached it, the storm continued to pound down on them the hardest rain any of them had ever felt. In front of the women, the waters were churning violently, causing their boat to rock wildly back and forth on the shoreline. The smell of the salty-sea air tingled the inside of their nostrils but, the typically scarce combination of anxiety and fortitude had them so preoccupied, they barely even noticed it.

By the time they reached the boat, four more women had died. All four ultimately died by electrocution from lightning but three of them were first wounded by quills. It was clear to everyone that the monsters and the weather were working together, under the command of Raum, to stall the women long enough for the lightning to strike and take their lives.

While the women struggled to untie the boat and push it off shore, two more of them were pierced by quills. One of them was instantly struck by another bolt of lightning but Jill and Elaine were able to pick the other woman up and carry her onto the boat before she could be killed.

As the boat left the shore, a short-lived feeling of relief set in. The women stared at the frightening monsters standing at the water's edge, allowing a small sense of victory to pass through their emotional web. Although the storm continued to rage and the waters continued their violent agitation, the monsters were no longer a threat.

Elaine stuck her tongue out while waving at the shoreline, sarcastically. "How do you like us now?" she yelled, needing to release her pent up anger and frustrations. "That's what I thought!"

As if Raum was responding to the taunt, the boat climbed the face of a wave and then snapped loudly down on the backside of it. The women were tossed forward in the boat and tumbled to the floorboards. It hurt but, fortunately, they managed to collect themselves fairly quickly. However, the reminder of the conditions instantly jolted the women back to reality. And, the reality of this situation was that Raum still had the upper hand.

~

Grant and the other men tried to settle into their boat; a smaller version of an early nineteenth century slave ship, also made entirely out of wood, without any of the elaborate trimmings or carvings. However, getting comfortable was virtually impossible in the middle of a blizzard. The air was freezing cold and visibility was fractious at best. If that wasn't sufficient to make the trip challenging enough, the water was absolutely frantic.

The men gathered below deck and briefly shared their sorrow over the men they had lost along the way. They then discussed the difficulties that still lie ahead. As the boat rocked and swayed wildly, cold water splashed inside through cracks and small holes. Discouragement swiftly took hold of the group.

Discouragement has the unique ability to both immobilize time and yet make it seem eternal. The men sat in silent uncertainty as if time was standing still. Grant considered trying to make a wise-crack to Max about the fact that Max had originally arrived in Kadosh wearing Bermuda shorts and flip-flops but this was a situation he just couldn't bring himself to make light of. The fear and apprehension that blanketed the room made that moment somehow feel like even though it had already lasted far too long, it still might never end.

The few moments that passed in silence, felt like hours. Silence can leave you alone with your thoughts, even in a room full of people. And, these were some dark thoughts.

~

"Raum won't let us get there," Will stated matter-of-factly. The statement both broke the silence and announced the miserable sentiment that had enveloped the entire room.

"We've come this far," Ray acknowledged in a half-hearted attempt to raise the collapsed spirits. "And we can't go back."

"All that means is that we're stuck," said a boy named Brett. "We're floating in the ocean in the middle of the worst storm I've ever seen in my life and, as if that wasn't enough to make me completely depressed, I can't swim. So, I'm a dead man."

"No, you're not," Kinsey insisted. "None of us are. At least not yet."

"It's just a matter of time," Brett insisted.

"I don't believe that."

"Of course you don't. You're probably a great swimmer."

"I'm an okay swimmer but, that has nothing to do with it,

Brett. I really believe that if we stick together, and keep our focus, we can make it."

"All of us?"

"I hope so. Look, I know it's been a hard journey. And, it's not going to get any easier before it's over. But, we can't go back now. And, even if we could go back, I wouldn't. I know it's been a long time for some of you but we have to remember what it's like to be with our families. Sure, there were bad times. We all had them. We wouldn't be here otherwise. But, there were also good times. Remember the big moments. Remember the little ones, too. Taking them for granted is how we got here in the first place. That has to end. Remember. Appreciate. Those moments aren't guaranteed to anyone. They're worth fighting for. That's why we started this journey. That's why we have to finish it. So, Brett can't swim. We'll just have to stay afloat."

"I tend to sink," Brett admitted.

"The boat, Brett. We'll have to keep the boat-"

"Raum isn't making it easy," Brett insisted.

"No, he isn't. But, neither are we. Let's keep pushing ahead."

"And go where exactly?" asked Will.

~

The inhabitants of each boat began to scan the ocean that

surrounded them. They lowered their heads into their shoulders and squinted their eyes to see through their individual storms. The blanket of weather made it difficult, but they kept looking for anything that would give them a sense of direction. Suddenly, they were each awarded a life-changing sight.

~

"Look," Zorica shouted, pointing.

Through their hurricane, they could see another storm. Lightning crashed down on the barely visible island in the South. It lit up the sky like fireworks on New Year's Eve.

"Over there too," exclaimed Sam, pointing at the white-covered North island.

"And there," called Whitney.

"Raum's attacking all four islands," Moirah realized out loud.

"Do you understand what that means?" proposed Tatum, a knowing smile playing on the corners of her lips.

"We're putting our families in jeopardy," Naomi stated sadly.

"We're not putting them in jeopardy," Tatum said. "They're putting themselves in jeopardy. We're all trying to reach each other."

The somber mood immediately transformed into an enthusiastic and unified, battle-ready euphoria as moans and tears of sorrow turned into shouts and tears of joy.

Tatum, with absolute jubilation, swiftly bellowed, "Let's start rowing!"

CHAPTER THIRTY
Joint Voyage

The boys rowed feverishly. The eye-opening experience of discovering that their families were fighting just as hard to get to them as they were had given them a sense of hope that had otherwise been lost for decades in this desperate world. They had been exhausted only moments ago but hope is the strongest fuel in existence and they suddenly found themselves with a full tank. No matter what happened next, they would never be the same. This place would never be the same either and every one of them knew it. The looming problem was the fact that Raum knew it, too. And, man was he angry.

But, the boys rowed on with reflections of their families from their minds increasing the power in their muscles. The thought of not wanting to be around his parents now seemed nearly impossible to Kinsey. *How could I have ever wanted to avoid them back home,* he wondered. He would sit in his room every night and barely speak to anyone but his sister. The truth is, it was discord that he was really avoiding. But, at the time, discord and his parents went hand in hand. Thankfully, none of that seemed to matter any longer.

After being faced with the reality of what it truly means to be completely separated from his family, there was nothing in this or any other world that he wanted more than to simply embrace each of them. Of course, his sister went without saying but now he also wanted to hug his parents with all the strength he had and tell them that he had never stopped loving them.

Simply put, he wanted his family back. Imperfections and all. And, this time, he knew they could be the unit they should have been all along. Adversity has a way of making people stronger, better versions of themselves. This was adversity on steroids. And, it was making the Snyders a stronger, better version of a family than they ever could have been otherwise.

This realization had sparked Kinsey's heartfelt, inspirational speech to the boys on his boat just moments ago. He meant it. He felt it. And, so did everyone else. Hope was now physically manifesting itself in every row of the oars Kinsey and the other boys firmly gripped.

Hope, like adrenaline, can cause people to do extraordinary things. There are moments when it can provide supernatural strength and endurance to those who would otherwise be weak and fatigued. This was, without a doubt, one of those moments. But, it wouldn't be the last moment of its kind that Kinsey would experience in Kadosh. In fact, the biggest was yet to come.

~

Tatum and the girls rowed with the same vigor as Kinsey and the boys. They were not in synch like a college rowing team would be but, they were working hard and looked more like a big group of young female Vikings – minus the furry hats.

The girls were too focused on the task at hand to have a conversation but, they were all flooded with anxious thoughts of the reunion that very well might be just hours away. Time and distance had turned resentment into tenderness and longing. Clearly, this was the complete opposite of the impact that Raum wanted to have. And his resulting wrath was on full display.

As the girls continued to fight back with their fierce rowing, Tatum could barely contain herself at the thought of giving Kinsey a big squeeze. Even in the moments when she wished she had some time to herself, she loved her brother dearly. And since this Kadosh adventure began, she had been given more time to herself than she wanted in her entire life. She could not wait to walk him home from school again. In that moment, she wished she could go home so their walks could begin again immediately and that they wouldn't ever grow up so that those walks could go on forever.

These were the thoughts that propelled every stroke of the oar as the girls' boat climbed the front of the giant waves, crested, and then plunged down the back of the same waves and into the next oceanic valley.

The high winds causing the waves were also pressuring the girls from all sides. The girls were extremely cold and wet, but that severe discomfort was now heavily outweighed by a determination so strong it created a tunnel vision effect that made everything else go virtually unnoticed.

~

The thunder was nearly deafening and lightning continued to violently strike the water around the women's boat as the storm chased after them like a gazehound tailing its game.

Water acts as a conductor. So, unlike when the lightning hit the ground, it was now striking and then immediately spreading out across the surface of the sea. The reflection of light off of the water amplified the effect and made it look even bigger and brighter than it actually was. Had it not been something they were afraid of, the women might have taken the time to appreciate just how beautiful and miraculous a sight was before them. Instead, it only added to the terror they were experiencing in that moment.

The fear that every strike produced set in motion a flinch from the women that interrupted the rowing pattern and caused further delay in reuniting them with their families. Each delay was quite brief, however. This was especially true for the mothers in search of their children. The bond a mom usually feels for her child is absolutely unparalleled and there were a lot of moms in this group. Each member of the group, however, was unwavering in her purpose and no weather or anything else, for that matter, would be able to stop them.

At least, that was their plan. Raum, of course, angry as ever, had plans of his own.

~

"How do we know the women are rowing toward us?" Max shouted his earnest question at Grant as the new fear took hold of the entire group.

"We don't," Grant answered honestly.

"What if we miss each other?"

"Then we change course, if we have to. But, we won't know until it happens."

"This boat can't survive out here in this weather for very

long."

"What other choice do we have?" Grant waited a moment, knowing full well there wasn't another choice and, therefore, no response was coming. He offered up the only suggestion he had, "We hope. We pray. We stick with the plan. Good enough?"

"Good enough," Max confirmed without allowing logical fear to creep in any further.

Safe from the worst of the snow itself, the men continued to row in freezing temperatures. Their muscles tightened and their bodies felt stiff but they rowed on, just as resolute as those with whom they were striving to reunite. They had survived cougars, rock monsters, and they were sure they would survive the snow and the sea.

This confidence was, sadly, a bit naïve. No one could have possibly known just how merciless, terrifying, and violent Raum's assault was about to get. But, they would all soon find out.

CHAPTER THIRTY-ONE
The Enemy's Grab Bag

With teeth chattering and bodies shivering, the men began to wonder if the temperature outside had dropped even further. The snow seemed to be getting heavier and even the hard work of rowing their big boat in aggressively turbulent waters couldn't keep them warm. They were not any less determined but, with outside forces getting stronger, the tunnel-vision level of focus they had was dwindling quickly.

The severe chill briefly reminded Grant of a camping trip he had once taken Kinsey on for some father and son bonding time. Kinsey was only five years old then, and it was his very first trip with just Dad. It was also his first experience camping because Jill had never cared for the experience herself. If Grant recalled correctly, he believed she had told him that human kind had advanced beyond sleeping on the dirt in the woods for a reason.

He nearly chuckled to himself as he realized how ironic a statement like that was in light of the situation they had found themselves in here in Kadosh.

Grant's mind took him back to the trip with Kinsey. There was a chill in the air then, too. Not nearly as biting as this one was but it had been strong enough to elicit some complaining from Kinsey, nonetheless. It was just the boys and Grant had been determined to turn his son into a permanent camping buddy. He tried his best to make it fun and, at first, Kinsey loved the event. Or, at least, he loved the idea of it.

Grant and Kinsey had awakened early that morning, loaded the truck, and headed up highway 2 toward Stevens Pass in the Cascade Mountains. They found a spot on the Skykomish River and did a little fishing before they even set up their campsite. They caught several Steelhead Trout that they would eat for dinner that night and everything seemed to be going according to Grant's master plan.

But as the sunlight was replaced by darkness and the noises of nature grew louder, Kinsey's fears set in. Grant did his best to distract his son by telling humorous stories over a delicious dinner.

Grant had cheated a little on the dinner and brought with him some barbecue sauce, butter, and a homemade dry rub to help him cook the Steelhead on the portable grill that he had also brought with them. Of course, he had also cheated a little on the dry rub, which was really just a store-bought seasoning salt that he had added lemon pepper and smoked paprika to. Cheating or not, the dinner was scrumptious. At least, Grant thought so. His five-year-old son, on the other hand, didn't eat a whole lot. He didn't laugh a whole lot at Grant's stories either.

However, if Kinsey's lack of appreciation for barbecued river fish and fears of wild animals and things that go bump in the night had been all that had gone wrong, they might have made it through the night. Unfortunately, an unexpected temperature drop in the evening became unbearable as the night went on because they were not remotely prepared for it on this early summer night. Kinsey got so cold he started crying and Grant was forced to pack everything up and take him home before spending a single night on what was supposed to be a four day and three night stay. Grant had never tried to take Kinsey camping again. *It's time to give that another shot*, Grant thought.

This was all just a fleeting memory and a short-lived thought for Grant as the men continued steadily – even when they experienced the first of the global earthquakes and the waters swelled into a tsunami wave train. The earthquakes were soon followed by underwater explosions caused by erupting volcanoes on the bottom of the ocean.

Raum had lost his temper.

Kinsey was the first to notice the circling sharks. Of course, like Kinsey had told Brett earlier, all they had to do was stay in the boat and they would be fine. However, the boat was rocking enough to make an old sea-pirate sick to his stomach and the boys were terrified they would be thrown overboard. Not the least of which, was the boy who couldn't swim, Brett.

Increasing their fear, other things began floating to the surface as well. The boys assumed that the strange fish they were seeing, both alive and dead, were rising up because of the underwater explosions they were experiencing and they were mostly right. However, many of them had also been called by Raum to wreak havoc on the boys for rebelling against him.

The variety of sea life was simultaneously fascinating and terrifying. They were getting an up-close and personal look at frilled sharks, cartilaginous fish, pelican eels, rattails, oarfish, fangtooths, dragonfish, and countless other bizarre deep-sea beasts. The colors were diverse but most were very dark. Some were even translucent and most had petrifying faces with piercing teeth that would scare the most fearless of people.

The bottom line was that they would do anything to keep themselves in that boat. Unfortunately, this would prove to be increasingly more difficult as Raum, of course, had the opposite goal in mind.

~

Lightning struck the bow of the boat, starting a fire, and the women went into panic mode. Doing their best to collect themselves in a hurry, they used hand-carved wooden bowls to scoop water from the scary creature-infested waters and poured it on the flames. They moved frantically, and Elaine nearly got her arm bitten off by a goblin shark but, eventually, they were able to put the fire out.

Lightning continued to strike and the women feared it would once again hit the boat and start another fire. If they weren't able to put the next one out, it could sink the ship and seal their fate.

Jill couldn't help but think they'd come too far to be stopped now. Success in this quest was, in her mind and the minds of the rest of the boat's operatives, more important than anything they had ever done or ever would do. Pressing on was the only option they had.

~

The waves encountered by Tatum and the rest of the girls were colossal. Every wave they climbed seemed like the face of

Everest - and then, the descent.

The ride was similar to the beginning of nearly every roller coaster ever created. The long, slow ascension was scary, but the crest - that pause before falling – now, that was terrifying. The fall itself was scary too but not nearly as much so as the anticipation that preceded it. The flip of the stomach at the crest of each wave was turning into an incurable nausea amongst the group. This pattern was extremely frightening and had continued much too long.

Tatum was the first to lose it and the chain-reaction that followed was a boat-wide mass puking of legendary proportions. Girls were projectile vomiting all over the boat and the waters around them. And the sea life began to feast.

The scene was beyond disgusting. But, it was also far from over and, unknown to them, the most daunting part of their entire seafaring adventure was just moments away.

CHAPTER THIRTY-TWO
The Perished

As the spewing subsided, the girls continued rowing. They were so determined to reach their families that they barely paid attention to the upchuck in their hair and on their clothes and skin.

When they had finally rowed past the vomit in the water, they noticed a milky-looking substance suddenly beginning to rise, in a whirlpool motion, toward the surface from the depths of the surrounding waters underneath their craft. The higher the substance got, the bigger it grew. It seemed slow at first. Deliberate and even cautious. But, that quickly changed. It was like a reverse funnel and it was ascending swiftly and increasing the span of its reach just as fast.

"What is that?" Zorica asked, peering over the side of the raft in the center of the girls' boat as the substance grew in circumference to a size wide enough to reach beyond the vessel's wingspan and began to lose shape.

"Looks like a giant jellyfish," commented Whitney with grim suspicion in her voice.

"That's no jellyfish," Tatum added just as gravely while watching whatever it was get closer by the second and feeling her curiosity shift to trepidation.

"Then what is it?"

"I have no idea but it's definitely not a jellyfish."

~

As the pearl-colored, free-flowing substance got close to the surface, it became clear that it wasn't a single creature but thousands of creatures traveling together. Whatever they were, they appeared to be both white and translucent and looked nearly human in shape.

"It almost looks like…like people," stated Max just before the creatures broke the surface on all sides of the boat, surrounding it like soldiers ready to break down the walls of a fort. What once appeared to be one creature had quickly been revealed as thousands of completely erratic creatures that were definitely humanoid in shape and size.

The worst part of watching the creatures break through the

surface of the water was the sound that came with it. The creatures were making a crying, moaning sound that reminded the men of a funeral. It was the same sound that people made as they grieved the loss of loved ones.

Grant had heard that sound when he lost his grandpa. Technically, it was his step-grandpa. His mother's biological father had passed away when she was a teenager and her mother remarried a man named Robert who everyone grew to call Poppa. He was beloved by the family and everyone missed him when he died. But the sound Grant was now hearing was familiar because it was the sound his Grammie made when she wept for the loss of her second husband. Only, now it was multiplied over and over again because of the sheer number of creatures that had risen from the depths of the sea that were now making it. The bemoaning sound was overwhelming. It was as if it caused a contagious sorrow that filled the hearts of everyone who heard it.

"Can't be," Grant began as he watched them start reaching for the boat and then slowly started to change his mind. "Can it? Oh, my…"

~

The fear the boys felt began to increase as they realized that these creatures were trying to get on the boat. They were crawling over each other, clawing and fighting their way to climb aboard.

"Take me with you," one of them said in a ghostly whisper that sent chills down the spines of the boys who heard it. This quickly caused a revelation in the collective minds of the boys. These creatures weren't sent to stop them; they came on their own accord to join them on their quest.

One voice turned into thousands as the wailing subsided and they all started begging the boys to let them come on board and finish the journeys they had started years ago. It quickly became clear that these creatures were the souls of boys just like them who had attempted to make this journey before and had failed.

~

The weight of this revelation was severe. Staring at the ghostly female forms in the water, Jill and the other women feared they were seeing their own destiny. It was horrifying because it was more than just possible; it was likely. Compassion set in and nearly overwhelmed them but it quickly gave way as the panic that first arrived at the sight of the milky white substance in the water returned swiftly and more fierce than ever.

"We should take them with us," Jill told Elaine.

"We can't," Elaine shot back. "It's too late for them."

"That's cold," Jill exclaimed.

"It's survival, Jill. They'd just capsize the boat. Do you want to end up like them?"

Surely the spirits didn't want to capsize the boat. They wanted the boat to reach the others. In fact, they wanted to be on it when it did. But, Elaine was still right. There were too many of them and trying to allow them to join the voyage would only ensure that the women on board would experience the same fate as the spirits had.

"They're us," Jill said quietly.

"Not if I can help it," Elaine said as she reached forward and pushed one of the women spirits back in the water.

The action felt totally cruel but it was absolutely necessary. The voices were getting louder and more jumbled together as the spirits climbed up the sides of the boat, fighting harder and harder for a chance to finish their own unsuccessful journey.

The women had no choice but to push them off. The effort seemed nearly futile, however, because the spirits outnumbered the living and they just kept coming. They had no intention of giving up. Surely, some of them had been fighting to reach their destination for hundreds of years. Maybe even more.

~

Kinsey pushed spirit after spirit off of the boat and back into the water as tears began streaming down his face. He wasn't alone in this. Many of the boys were having a similarly emotional reaction to the situation they found themselves in.

The tears were caused by a combination of guilt and the weight of the fact that dying in this place was a conclusive matter being, quite literally, right in their face. It was all simply too much to keep inside. The truth is, it would be too much for anybody.

The fact that dying in Kadosh remained final was something they all knew but hadn't fully come to grips with until now. These spirits exposed the harsh reality that if the boys failed on this journey, the results would be eternal. That was an emotionally heavy thing to acknowledge. And, now, they didn't have a choice but to face it head on, and all of the emotions that came with it.

Although the spirits of the boys who had perished would never see their families again, it wasn't too late for Kinsey and his friends. They fought back and fought hard to make sure they wouldn't die here. Unfortunately, they fought with no idea that what Raum had in store for them next would undoubtedly end the journey for a number of them and force them to join the spirits in the abyss below.

CHAPTER THIRTY-THREE
The Final Assault

Kinsey and the others were fighting hard but losing the battle as they continued to push the spirits of the boys who had perished off the boat. There were just too many of them and they were absolutely relentless. Brett, realizing his worst fear, was pulled overboard because too many of the spirits were trying to use him to pull themselves up onto the deck. He screamed and splashed around briefly but, in what barely felt like an instant, he sank below the surface, silencing his scream, and was gone.

The fight on board appeared useless. But, suddenly, the landscape began to change. The waters around the boat started to recede, pulling countless spirits away and swallowing them up. Those who weren't pulled away immediately were fought off by the boys and tossed back into the ocean to be swallowed up as well.

The emotional roller coaster continued as the fear subsided and guilt returned. They stared into the depth as the milky white substance grew smaller and ultimately disappeared in just the opposite manner from which it had arrived. As a group, the boys were silent and motionless as they experienced a bit of relief. But, none of that would last either.

"Is that land?" Andy questioned out loud.

Kinsey turned to look and, sure enough, they saw land. The jubilation was as brief as Brett's screams. They quickly realized that they had traveled so far that the island in the center of the other four, the place where Raum was said to dwell, was actually in sight. Raum's island was now the closest piece of dry land but it certainly wasn't where they wanted to go.

Back at camp, they had originally decided they would set sail for the North island where the men were. But, once they discovered that their loved ones were all setting sail as well, they might have adjusted their course had things been calmer. Instead, they had been set on escaping the madness and hoping to find their loved ones at sea. Unfortunately, this allowed the storm to force them toward Raum's island. They feared this was Raum's plan all along and their fate could be mere moments away.

~

The waters seemed to have receded into three separate whirlpools several hundred feet away from different sides of the men's boat. Suddenly, the holes filled back up from the bottom, but not with water. And, not with a milky white substance either.

This time, the substance was much darker. It was a crimson red with blotches of deep blue scattered all over it that, from a distance, made it look like a rising ocean floor that had been bloodied by the deaths caused by Raum. But, just as the milky white substance had proven itself to be something more complex, this would be no different.

Bursting out of all three whirlpools were gargantuan spiraling sea monsters. They shot completely out of the water like giant dolphins, giving the men a good, albeit fleeting, look at the bizarre creatures. They had enormous serpent-like bodies and giant bulbous heads.

Before touching back down in the water, they sprawled out their long and scaly tentacles. This gave them a spider-like appearance.

"Is that a squid?" asked Max.

"Biggest squids on earth don't come in that size," answered Grant.

"I'm not sure we're on earth. Are you?"

"Yep," admitted Grant. "That's a good point. I don't know where we are either. But, I still don't think those are squid."

"Then what are they?" shouted Max in utter fear as the monsters finally made enormous splashes in the water.

"I don't know but they're headed right for us!" Grant shouted back as the monsters repositioned themselves and immediately sped toward the boat like enormous torpedoes. "Brace yourselves!"

~

The gigantic monsters collided with the boat on all three sides, crushing and almost immediately capsizing it. The women were tossed in all directions as if they'd been in a horrible head-on collision on a major freeway. But, instead of landing on pavement, they all found themselves in the water. Not that the water felt like a soft landing. Some of them were tossed so high in the air that hitting the water almost felt like hitting the ground as their bodies slapped and thudded before piercing the surface. Their lungs quickly filled with water. In an instant, the women were gasping for air and then anxiously swimming in the dangerous waters, with severe angst over all the creatures they'd seen – especially the massive things that had just put them there.

Jill knew that Raum's island was potentially as dangerous as these waters and anything they'd been through already. But, at this moment, the fact that these waters and all of the creatures in them were present and real while Raum's island was merely a terrifying theory, made the island seem like the safer place. She swam toward it with all the strength she could muster.

Hearing screaming, crying, and the splashing sounds of other women swimming just as hard as she was, Jill tried to ignore the noise but couldn't and it all brought tears pouring out of her eyes. These cries were different than the ones the spirits had made. They weren't cries of grief, but of absolute terror. And, Jill began to add to the sounds as she swam for her life.

Out of the corner of her eye she saw a bull shark bite into a woman and pull her under water about 8 feet away. Through what had now turned into sobbing, Jill began to pray. *Oh, God, please help me reach that island.*

~

Tatum could feel herself growing more tired with every stroke. She felt as though she had been swimming for hours. Luckily, she could see land and it was getting closer.

Suddenly, she felt something wrap around her body and sting her. It was painful and she had to stop swimming to see what it was.

She looked behind her and just below the surface of the water she saw a Lion's Mane Jellyfish. It was nearly twice her size and it had wrapped one of its 120 foot-long tentacles around her, injecting her with venom through thousands of microscopic barbed stingers.

The throbbing sensation was intense. She fought hard but it wouldn't let go. All she could do was turn and keep swimming. In spite of the pain, her adrenaline gave her all the energy she needed and she swam until she hit land. The jellyfish must've hit land too because something finally caused it to let go.

She pulled herself up out of the water and onto the shoreline. Tatum grimaced out of pain. Her skin was covered in a red rash. She wanted to grab the part that hurt but her entire body was stinging in pain and she couldn't grab everything at once. Instead, she stretched her arms out and grabbed handfuls of sand. She squeezed it through her fingers and finally let out a big breath of air.

Slowly, her eyes opened. The pain wasn't gone but distraction can be a strong medicine. Tatum looked around as a new fear set in. She had reached Raum's island.

PART SEVEN
The Gathering

CHAPTER THIRTY-FOUR
Yin

Raum's island was surprisingly small and almost perfectly square. There was no living vegetation and no sign of life beyond the beach. It was mountainous terrain but the boulders were jagged black lava rock and the bushes and trees that had once been alive looked like they had been burned in a fire a long time ago, making the island an eerily dark and desolate place.

~

Jill looked down the shoreline as several women crawled out of the ocean. Her sobbing had subsided as she scanned the water and saw only one straggler, quickly realizing that the dozen and a half women she saw were the only ones who had made it.

She lowered her head, wanting to cry again but failing to find the energy to release more than a single additional tear, which slid down her cheek and disappeared in the wet sand below. She felt thankful for surviving and yet guilty at the same time. She was saddened by the faces that flashed through her mind. They were faces of women she had come to know in this place. Women who had now perished and joined the milky white substance in the abyss just a few football fields from where she was sitting, alive and safe. At least for now.

As the women started to gather together, the fear caused by the realization of where they now found themselves began welling up and replacing the sadness inside of Jill. *Will Raum finally show himself?* she wondered. *Is this where the rest of us will die? Was this journey a mistake?* She had so many questions and virtually no answers – only fears and angst.

She barely noticed that the sand on this beach seemed to sink a little deeper than any other sand she had ever walked on. Perhaps it was just the weight of the situation on her proverbial shoulders. Whatever it was, she felt heavy and low. This place felt bleak and grim. The hope she felt when she saw that people from the other islands were on the same journey she and the other women were on, had all but gone out of her like oxygen after a solid punch to a wide open and totally unprepared gut.

"What do we do now?" asked Diane as she and Elaine approached Jill from opposite directions.

"I have no idea," Elaine answered.

"Let's get to one of the other sides and find out if we can see what happened to the men and children," Jill suggested anxiously.

~

Leading the girls up the embankment, Tatum was terrified at what she might find. She could be encountering additional menacing beasts sent by Raum. She could be meeting Raum, himself, face-to-face. Or, worse, she could look out at the ocean and discover that her entire family was dead. Her body began to quiver and she was convinced it had nothing to do with being cold and wet. What she couldn't possibly know was that at the same time, her mom was experiencing the same feeling of anxiety and lost hope. Thankfully, that was all about to change.

~

As Grant reached the top of the bank and stepped out onto more level ground, he surveyed the sinister environment. He had never seen anything like it before. It was almost as if he was standing in front of nature's gothic castle.

"Who is that?" asked Max.

Grant quickly looked in the direction Max was pointing and

saw someone climbing up the east bank. He squinted, trying to see, and then his eyes widened and filled with tears of gladness. His entire body began to tingle with joy as he realized who it was, "Kinsey."

~

"Dad," Kinsey stated under his breath with glee as he started to run enthusiastically toward his father.

Suddenly, fear gave way to jubilation as people were running from all four sides of the island. Not only was Kinsey running from the East but also the rest of the boys followed him as they saw members of their own families. The same was true of the men from the North, the women from the South, and the girls from the West. The smiles on their faces seemed to be untamable until the moment turned.

Before any of them had reached the others, everyone was forced to stop when the ground began to shake. Kinsey's first thought was another earthquake. He'd already experienced several of those today. But, this seemed smaller and more localized. That's when he finally noticed the hideous smell saturating the island. It was like the most foul, rotten garbage he'd ever smelled. As the ground shook, the smell got worse as if a garbage can lid was slowly being lifted and the stench of the grime beneath it was seeping out because the filth itself was slowly being revealed. It finally dawned on him, *We're about to encounter Raum.*

In the very center of the island, separating everyone once again, the black lava rock burst open and Raum shot out of it. The rocky terrain crumbled all around him and he landed on the ground with a loud thud, shaking the floor again with his weight.

He was hideous. Dark like the island's boulders, his body seemed to be made up of slithering serpents. He was large and powerful like the rock monsters, but even bigger. He had moss hanging all over him like the forest beasts, and spewing from his circular mouth which bore thousands of long, pointed teeth, was the most violent noise that Kinsey had ever heard. Raum even displayed his own pair of wings made up of the same type of inflorescences but much larger than those of the monster the girls had faced. Each wing was made up of thousands of small, black, star-shaped flowers that appeared to have snakes slithering through them.

It was as if he represented all of the nastiest parts of everything he had thrown at the men, women, boys and girls to stop their journey. Or, perhaps, each of those monsters represented a different part of his revolting being.

But, there were also attributes that were uniquely his own. The most distinguishable of which were five pointed horns growing out of his head. The one above his forehead was the largest and most prominent. It stuck straight out and was flanked on either side by smaller horns that went in the opposite direction. The other two were on the side of his head. These were the smallest and they also protruded forward.

Not someone you want to butt heads with, Kinsey briefly thought to himself before his mind quickly snapped back to the seriousness of the situation. He glanced around at the boys in his vicinity. They were all covering their noses to try and filter the horrendous stench but they couldn't keep their eyes off of Raum, the hideous demon separating them from their families. *Now, what?*

The sound emanating from Raum's violently disgusting head meant business. Without words, it announced everyone as trespassers who had escaped their prisons and invaded his island. It was clear that he was now determined to wipe them out once and for all.

CHAPTER THIRTY-FIVE
Yang

In the same way that smaller measuring cups fit into larger measuring cups like Russian nesting dolls, or the way that young children are little versions of their parents, life is one big journey made up of a lot of smaller journeys. Each individual journey is filled with moments like vehicles that take a person to their destination. Everyone ends up somewhere. The mystery comes in whether they end up there by accident or on purpose. Often it appears to be a little of both. This was no exception.

The sight, sound, and sheer presence of Raum had resulted in a gripping sense of terror that had now completely overwhelmed everyone. Everyone but Kinsey, that is. Of course, he was scared. Who wouldn't be? But, he suddenly realized that he had survived everything this Raum had thrown at him. They all had. Well, not everyone. But, he and everyone that was standing in that place, at that moment, facing Raum. Somehow, in spite of the nightmare playing out in front of him, Kinsey felt just a hint of confidence. It stemmed from the realization that his entire family had cared enough to endure such a dangerous expedition in order to try to find each other. It brought a hope that can only come from loving and being loved and it was enough to give Kinsey an extraordinary moment of courageous behavior.

Courageous behavior can be displayed by big actions like leaping in front of a bullet or running into a burning building to save a life. It can also be displayed in small actions like this one: Kinsey simply took a step forward. He was the only one who dared to approach the ferocious, evil monster in front of him.

And, Raum noticed.

Raum turned toward Kinsey with uncontrollable hell and fury shooting out of every pore. With a howl of rage, he raised a fist and panic struck the helpless crowd of people. The most terrified, of course, were Grant, Jill and Tatum. Raum was about to strike down with a fireball of vengeance against the small boy when suddenly, before anyone even had time to react, extremely bright sunshine seemed to crack open the dark sky and the blinding light surprised them all. Even Raum was caught off guard, bringing any destructive action to a halt.

A stormy wind rushed down over the island and a great cloud

with intense brightness around it descended out of the sunshine. Hovering above the island, the cloud had fire flashing forth continually with gleaming metal in the midst of it as if an invisible blacksmith was forging something inside the great fires.

Everyone, including Raum and Kinsey, looked upward, curiously. The light continued to get even brighter until Raum and every single person on the island was forced to turn away. No one could withstand the imposing brightness.

No one, but once again, save Kinsey.

For Raum, it was primarily fear that made it unbearable. Raum was the only one present who knew exactly where and what the light was coming from. That knowledge made him turn away and tremble. Light, after all, exposes the darkness. The dark can no longer exist in the presence of light. So, Raum had every right to be very afraid. The only one who could have seen Raum's trepidation was Kinsey and he was too fascinated by what he saw in the sky to pay any attention to Raum even though he would have enjoyed watching him quiver.

For everyone else, it was just too bright to keep their eyes open. But, for them, the warmth that it brought was comforting and magnificent in both an inviting and somehow regal way. It was like a starving pauper being asked to dine at the majestic royal table by the King himself. Somehow, the light brought with it a sense of joy and relief that no one in Kadosh had ever felt in such a strong capacity.

Kinsey managed to look on. He saw four living creatures appear from inside of the cloud. They had a human likeness but each had four faces and four wings.

Each creature had both a human face and the face of an eagle. These faces were flanked on the right by the face of a lion and on the left by the face of an ox.

The two wings that were spread out on each creature touched the wings of another. The creatures also had wings at their side, covering their bodies and human hands barely visible underneath. Their legs were straight with no knees and their feet had soles like that of a calf. Kinsey briefly wondered how they moved without joints in their legs. He was so awestruck by the creatures that the thought left him quickly as he simply looked on in amazement.

The skin of the creatures was beautiful. It gleamed and sparkled like burnished bronze. They were like nothing Kinsey had ever seen before and nothing he had ever seen was more elegant and striking than these creatures staring down at him from the cloud.

As the creatures began to move, Kinsey had forgotten to even pay attention to how they did it. Clearly, these phenomenal beings didn't need joints in their legs. There was something altogether special about what they were and how they did everything.

They darted to and fro like the appearance of a flash of lightning. It looked as though they reached into the fires with their human hands to pull something out as if they were retrieving something they came to deliver. But, as the lightning strike flashes increased with every move, the light became so intense that not even Kinsey could continue to look upon it.

Tatum then took notice of the warmth emanating from the light, which gave a similar feeling to sitting at the perfect distance from a roaring fireplace as the comforting warmth enveloped her. It was a feeling she hoped would never come to an end.

Kinsey, with his eyes now shut, suddenly recognized the disappearing odor of Raum's island and the fact that it was being replaced by a scent somehow both foreign and familiar, like a combination of wonderfully exotic spices. It was so brilliant, he wished he could bottle it and share it with the whole world.

Although everyone's eyes were closed and they couldn't see it, hovering in front of each of them, was a watermelon-sized sphere made up entirely of light. These lights had obviously traveled together, like a flock of birds, creating one formation and the appearance of one massive light. But, now, having been delivered by the creatures in the cloud of fire, they were there for a group purpose and that purpose was a series of singular assignments.

Slowly extending from each light, appeared what could only be described as arms. They reached forward and touched the individual people with reassurance that filled them with a confidence and a peace that would seem ludicrous to anyone looking at the situation from an outside perspective because of what the people faced. As the light touched each person, they also very carefully, and without anyone realizing what was happening, armed them for battle.

CHAPTER THIRTY-SIX
The Last Battle Begins

Without any warning at all, every bit of the lights, the cloud and its fire, the four beautiful creatures, and the comforting warmth they all brought with them, vanished into thin air and were gone without any trace. They also took with them the pleasant aroma that had masked the outlandish stench that otherwise blanketed Raum's barren wasteland of an island.

As everyone noticed the abrupt change in the atmosphere on their skin, the sudden lack of bright light through their eyelids, and the unfortunate conversion of scent in their nostrils, they also perceived an alteration in the weight on their bodies. Opening their eyes, they slowly discovered they had been outfitted with armor. They now all had rock-hard breastplates on their chests, tight belts around their waists, new sturdy shoes on their feet, solid helmets on their heads, dense shields in one hand and sharp swords in the other. The light had disappeared, which could have been a major disappointment, but one thing it didn't take with it was the sense of awe it had caused in Kadosh with its visitation. What it left behind was such a blessing that no one felt a single iota of disappointment in the fact that it hadn't stayed. Every person on that island looked themselves over, then glanced around at their fellow soldiers, and the confident peace they had been given by the light grew exponentially.

A crisis doesn't build something new within a person. It simply reveals what that person is already made of. Kinsey had shown what he was made of moments ago when he stepped forward to face Raum. The journey as a whole, and especially the moment they now found themselves in, was revealing exactly what was inside of every man, woman, boy and girl facing Raum along with Kinsey. Now armed for battle, it had already become quite clear in each individual's mind exactly what had to be done next. The final battle on this journey was about to officially begin.

As everyone looked up at Raum, the equally bleak and repugnant monster looked back down at them. He scanned the prisoners turned soldiers in front of him and probably would have displayed an arrogant smile at the thought of the fight that was coming, if he was capable of smiling. He was pleased that the light had not stayed to fight but, instead, had chosen to trust these people to do battle. He was sure the light had made a mistake and, as a result, his self-confidence level was peaking.

Raum's slithering arms reached down and his massive hands lifted giant rocks off the ground. He raised them up as he opened his repulsive mouth and discharged his vehement roar.

Raum hurled the first boulder at his new arch-nemesis, Kinsey Snyder. Fortunately, Kinsey leapt out of the way just in the nick of time. It hurt as he hit the stony ground but he was thankfully safe. At least, he was safe for the time being. The real danger was just getting started.

As rocks were tossed in every direction, the men, women, boys and girls all had to take cover behind their shields. Some were completely protected from the boulders hitting with explosive force while others were knocked tumbling backwards like pins in a bowling alley. They each bounced hard and the ones who survived were still getting cut up and bruised.

The boulders Raum was throwing clearly had the potential to cause a lot of pain through injury. But, even more serious, they had the potential to kill. They were hard and heavy so, of course they could crush a person. Or, at least, a part of a person that would include a vital organ like the heart or the brain. But, beyond crushing, they could also break bones and make it impossible for someone to keep moving. They were additionally sharp and jagged and could produce deep wounds that could cause a person to bleed until his or her brain wouldn't work and their heart stopped beating.

There were no medics on this battlefield. No helicopters to pick someone up and take them to a hospital or, at the very least, a safe place to try and heal. On this battlefield, if someone got hurt badly, he or she would most likely die.

Grant felt grief set in as he looked to his left and saw a man lying just four or five yards away. The man had clearly been struck by one of Raum's boulders and Grant could only assume, was now dead. He was briefly encouraged when he saw the man take a breath but, the relief was fleeting because the next breath the man took was a deep gasp and ended up being his last. Discouragement would have been the easy path but Grant and most of the others chose determination instead. The people that had died, and would still die, Grant and the others determined, would not die in vain. Their deaths would have purpose because they would allow others to succeed, and that is exactly what they intended to do.

Raum was clearly more powerful than any one of them. But, they outnumbered him. The trick would be in figuring out how to act on their strength and his weakness. At this moment, they had him surrounded but, he had them playing defense and they needed an offensive attack.

"We need to get closer," Tatum shouted to Zorica.

"Closer?" Zorica yelled back in shock. "Are you kidding

me?"

"It's the only way to strike!"

"Strike how? Strike where?"

"With whatever we've got and wherever we can! Let's move!" Tatum turned to Moirah and signaled her to follow before sprinting toward Raum. Zorica and Moirah both followed her lead, ducking out of the way and behind their shields as necessary when crashing stones struck the ground and shattered nearby like grenades throwing shrapnel all around them.

"Look!" Ray shouted as he pointed toward the girls.

Kinsey poked his head over his shield and spotted them inching closer to Raum. "They're moving in on him," Kinsey yelled. "Let's get him from our side!"

Ray and the other boys followed Kinsey's lead. Soon, the men and women were moving toward Raum as well. The closer everyone got, the angrier Raum became. He was breathing fire through his nostrils as he continued to throw the rocks and bellow that same atrocious sound.

Finally, as Raum accepted the fact that he was outnumbered, he threw the last of his rocks and spread his massive, menacing wings as he bellowed the most violent noise anyone on the island had ever heard. He flapped his wings a couple of times to get himself off of the ground. But, what happened next was the most astonishing part. He retracted, balled himself up, and fell to the ground where he landed with a giant thud and broke apart.

The break was purposeful though which didn't take long to become evident as the men, women, girls and boys watched his parts spring into action. This was Raum's way of disassembling.

Confusion set in as everyone realized they had gone from facing Raum as one barbarous giant, to facing Raum as all of his grotesque parts. Now they were the ones confronting numbers far greater than their own and every single person was surrounded by swarming throngs of beasts.

CHAPTER THIRTY-SEVEN
The War Concludes

The monster's leaves fanned out as it opened its mouth, spreading out its sharp teeth, to let out a brutal screech when Tatum stabbed it in the belly. As her blade sunk deeply into the beast, Tatum turned it to the left and then back to the right, making sure that it had the full effect she needed it to have. Tatum pulled her sword out and struck it again, this time a bit higher in the middle of the chest, before turning to face another oncoming beast. Behind her, she didn't see the black mist slither away from the slain monstrosity when it died.

Kinsey swung his sword through the air and decapitated the earthy beast before him. Unlike his sister, he stopped long enough to watch the black mist immediately slither away as the body quickly turned to a pile of yard waste like the others of its kind had before it. It all happened so quickly and Kinsey was too involved in the battle to think about the implications of what he had just seen. He turned just in time to save himself from an attack by stabbing another snarling beast between its forelegs and into its heart. He then promptly watched the same type of black mist slither across the ground toward the giant hole that Raum had exploded out of earlier.

Scanning the battle scene all around him, he watched his mother jab her sword into the back of a slinky creature. He saw his family and the others around them winning the battle. As they did, he also noticed that the strange black mist seeping into Raum's crater was happening with each and every creature they killed. It looked like shadows being sucked underground by an invisible vacuum. These few seconds were just enough time for Kinsey to finally realize that the black mist was the pieces of Raum's spirit that had been divided up among the many creatures that were now fighting his battle. And, the implication of this realization was that Kinsey and the others were actually beating Raum one beast at a time.

"Kill them all!" Kinsey shouted at everyone who would listen. "Kill them all!"

The response was a roar akin to a battle cry that energized the troops with vigorous intensity. Kinsey grinned as he raised his sword to continue fighting. The grin didn't come from enjoying the fight or feeling proud of his violent triumphs. It was a grin that came from a very pure place. It was based in unification and love. These were things he hadn't felt in a long time and probably never so strongly. He loved his family and he knew that his family loved him. Amazingly, in that moment, Kinsey actually felt thankful for the hell he had been through in Kadosh.

It was in that very moment that Kinsey Snyder learned a lesson that would benefit him for the rest of his life. He would remember this moment fondly for exactly that reason. It was a lesson that few people ever fully grasp in their entire lifetime. Kinsey had been given the opportunity, and seized it, to learn this lesson at the age of nine. He couldn't possibly know it but the lesson had a lot to do with the Yin and Yang theory that Kinsey's dad had discussed with his friend Max.

The tough stuff that people go through, the really hard stuff that everyone wishes they could avoid, is meant to be appreciated every bit as much as the stuff that everyone enjoys so easily. The times when life is difficult, when we suffer loss or hardship; those are the times that make the good times stand out.

A blue piece of paper wouldn't stand out if placed in a room painted in the same color of blue. But, if you put that piece of paper in a completely white room, it would suddenly jump out at you so that you could appreciate its full beauty. The same is true of the things we love.

In the case of the Snyders, it had taken the experience of life without each other to make them appreciate just how much they loved one another. The same was true for everyone who had made this journey to Raum's island with them. Life in Kadosh had been an arduous experience for all of them, but the love they now recognized as a result of it, made the arduous experience worthy of their deep appreciation.

But, the lesson Kinsey learned in that moment is a lesson that transcends family and relationships. It's true in all of life. We can't appreciate the gift of just simply being without understanding the consequences of death. We don't fully appreciate kindness until we've been bullied or just plain beaten down by the difficulties of life. We wouldn't know love or loyalty in its full capacity if we hadn't first experienced hate or betrayal. Simply put, it takes the bad stuff to make sure that we can recognize the good. Knowing that truth makes the hard times bearable.

This was an extreme version of one of those very times and Kinsey had begun to truly appreciate it. That appreciation would only grow over time. It would grow tremendously, not just for Kinsey, but for each and every one of them.

The battle raged on and not everyone survived but more did than didn't. And when those who made it watched the last piece of Raum's spirit slither away and back into the ground, they cheered victoriously. Men, women, girls and boys all high-fived and hugged one another for a few seconds and then quickly realized they could finally reunite with their families. One by one, they all started their exuberant sprint toward one another.

The reunion could not have been more ideal if a symphony had been hired to play and the crescendo had taken place at the very moment that everyone embraced.

Tatum was the first to reach Kinsey. Their love for each other poured out with the hug. They didn't even notice the reunions going on all around them as people like Elaine and Moirah held each other and sobbed. They did, however, feel a warm breeze begin to course through the island as an auspicious energy began to bubble around each individual family reunion.

Grant was the next to arrive and he took his children in his arms like a proud soldier returning home to his family from a great war. He had never loved anything more than he loved his family at that very moment.

The cozy breeze turned into a strong but inviting wind as the Snyder family circle was completed with Jill's arrival and her embrace with each one of her family members stirred a passion that she had never felt before. The moment was quite simply perfect.

CHAPTER THIRTY-EIGHT
Home

When the Snyders opened their eyes, they slowly realized that they were holding each other in the forest near their home. They were crouched down in the same area where they had all disappeared. But, most importantly, where they had vanished in pieces, they had now returned as a whole family.

"No way," Tatum exclaimed.

"We're back," Grant added in astonishment.

"We are," Jill enthusiastically agreed.

They stood up, arms still encircling one another, and glanced around. As they took in the familiar sights and scents of the world they had returned to, their joy and elation swelled to overflowing. They had left this world and entered Kadosh, carrying with them so much baggage full of pain, anger and bitterness. But they left that dark and dreary world and returned to this familiar place with their hearts packed full of love, harmony and peace. This world wasn't any different than they had left it. But, they had returned changed.

"Let's go home," Grant finally said. In that moment, it didn't even cross his mind that he had previously dreaded every moment spent at home. All he could think about was how thrilled he now was to be headed back there with his family. It had been months, maybe even years since it had been a place he actually wanted to be. Now, it was the only place he wanted to be.

The family started walking through the forest with a unified pep in their step. They looked like a team for the first time in years. They walked in silence for a moment until Kinsey asked the question that was on all of their minds, "That really happened, right?"

"It must have," Jill answered. "We all experienced it. We did all experience it, didn't we?"

"Yeah," Tatum agreed while her father nodded his head affirmatively.

"True," Kinsey matched the response but did so ponderously.

Bringing the conversation back to this world, Tatum exclaimed, "I cannot begin to describe the way I've missed real food. Should I call in an order?"

"Actually," Jill said, "I was thinking we could scrape

something up in the kitchen together."

"That sounds good," Tatum responded with a smile.

"What're you making?" asked Grant.

"We'll see what we've got," Jill explained. "Not much as I recall. Actually, we'll probably have to hit the store. And, what do you mean 'you'? When I said we should scrape something up together, I meant all four of us."

"If I'm helping," Grant sighed, "I hope it's microwaveable."

"We'll find something for you to do," Tatum told her dad. "I'm assuming you can stir, right?"

"I can probably manage," Grant said with a grin.

Another moment of silence passed as Kinsey continued to ponder the experience of their journey. Finally, he had to let another question out. "So, what does everyone think? Is Raum still alive?"

No one answered right away because no one was sure exactly what the correct answer was.

Finally, Grant responded laboriously, "Well, we definitely killed the body but that dark spirit may still exist. And, by the way, I think your bravery is what made it possible to stop Raum, tough guy," Grant said while rubbing Kinsey's head.

Kinsey liked the attention but shook it off anyway. "I don't think it was me. I think it was all of us. I think we were finally together the way we always should have been. I'm pretty sure that's what brought the light and the light is really what made it possible."

"You just might be right. Tough and smart." Grant squeezed his son's shoulder proudly as they walked up the steps to their house.

"We might have to go back, you know." Kinsey stated nonchalantly, stopping everyone else in their tracks.

"Excuse me?" Jill asked in total bewilderment.

"Well, there are still a lot of people in Kadosh. Someone has to show them the way out. I think that might be our responsibility now."

As they stepped inside, a tulip in the garden turned to watch them enter and widened its petals as if smiling approvingly at Kinsey.

Meanwhile, Tatum and her parents all looked at each other apprehensively, knowing full well that Kinsey was absolutely and terrifyingly right. At nine years old, Kinsey had already learned more than most people learn in an entire lifetime.

While the eyes of the light were still clearly on the Snyder family, so were the eyes of the dark. Outside of the line of vision from anyone, a withered licorice fern planted in the Snyders unattended garden, shrunk down into an earthy-bodied badger type of creature and burrowed into the ground, off to warn Raum of the Snyder's pending return.

Remaining oblivious to the presence of anything from the world they had visited, the Snyders followed Kinsey inside of their house to plan dinner together.

What a wonderfully interesting boy, Grant thought.

—The—
Four Corners

C.S. Elston

F—The—
Four Corners

Reader's Guide

1. Before Kadosh, the Snyder family included both good relationships and bad ones. Which would you put in each category and why? What have been some of your best and worst relationships?

2. Why does Kinsey live such an isolated life? Have you missed out on things in your own life for similar reasons?

3. When the story starts, the Snyder family has mostly good memories from their past but things have taken a bad turn in the last few years. How have each of the characters responded?

4. Tatum is described as someone who can make lemonade out of the lemons life gives her. Can you think of times when you or someone you know have been able to make the best out of a negative situation?

5. Do you agree or disagree with the statement: "The weight of sorrow is incalculable but, if it could be measured, it might be the heaviest substance on earth." and why or why not? Can you think of examples of times when sorrow has truly weighed you down?

6. What was the emotional catalyst that allowed Raum to take the Snyder family out of the world they knew and place them in Kadosh?

7. In Kadosh, some people are willing to journey out and try to find their families and others choose to stay behind. In both the story and in life, what do you think drives some people to make their situations better? What do you think holds others back? Which type of person do you relate to more?

8. The binding nature of Yin and Yang is a strong theme in "The Four Corners" – particularly in the second half. Can you see elements of that in your own life?

9. Do you agree or disagree with the statement: "Hope is the strongest fuel in existence. . ." and why or why not? Can you think of times when hope has given you the energy you needed to persevere in a difficult situation?

10. Grant and Jill's priorities change drastically in Kadosh. Have you ever encountered a situation that completely transformed your outlook?

11. Kinsey came out of his shell in Kadosh and his courage peaks when he faces Raum. What is the most courageous thing you have ever done? Have you ever found strength you didn't know you had just when you needed it the most?

12. Early in the story, Tatum promises Kinsey that they will always find a way to stay together. Have you ever made a promise that was next to impossible to keep? Were you able to keep it?

13. Grant finds home the most desirable place he can think of by the end of the story. But, when the story begins, it is the last place he wants to be. Have you ever been in a situation where something transformed that drastically for you?

14. What do you think life and home is like for the Snyders after the story ends?

15. Do you think the Snyders will return to Kadosh? Why or why not?

Also by C.S. Elston

Now Available:

"The Gift of Tyler"

"The Gift of Rio"

Available June, 2020:

"The Four Corners of Darkness"

Coming Soon:

"The Four Corners of Winter"

"The Gift of Matias"

"The Gift of Amanda"

After award-winning stage work in the nineties, Chris Elston moved to Los Angeles where he wrote more than two dozen feature film and television screenplays. He has been invited to participate in screenwriting events for Cinema Seattle and Angel Citi Film Festival. In 2013, Chris left Los Angeles for the suburbs of his hometown, Seattle, Washington, to get married and start a new chapter in his own story. Five and a half years later, the journey of the chapter that followed landed he and his wife in Prescott, Arizona where they now reside.

Made in the USA
Middletown, DE
20 August 2020